Geronimo Must Die
Copyright© 2017 J. R. Lindermuth
Cover Design Livia Reasoner
Sundown Press
www.sundownpress.com

SUNDOWN PRESS

All rights reserved.
ISBN-13: 978-1544076515
ISBN-10: 1544076517

Dedication: For my Dad,
who loved a good Western.

GERONIMO MUST DIE

J. R. Lindermuth

Kathleen,
Thanks for all
your support.
Best,
J. R. Lindermuth

Gibbous MOON

Chapter 1

The first shot raised a cloud of dust between our feet. Flinging myself against Geronimo, I knocked him to the ground and covered his body with my own. The second shot struck and crackled into the framework of the wickiup. After a moment of silence and no more shots, Geronimo barked, "Get off me, fool."

I complied. We rose, surrounded by a crowd of muttering warriors who'd been summoned by the shooting. The rifle fire came from a bluff above the camp and a number of men hurried off in that direction. They wouldn't find the sniper. Having failed in his mission, I knew he was long gone.

For the second time, I'd saved Geronimo's life. He seemed no more grateful than he had the first time. Brushing himself off, he inquired if those within the wickiup were unharmed. Assured of the safety of his family, he turned to me. "Why are you here?"

Sieber had sent me. A fool's mission, though I hadn't told him so. I learned a long time ago not to argue with Al Sieber.

Dawn on a frosty morning. Steam rising from the coats of the horses in the corrals. The boys watching the horses huddled with their arms clasped around themselves or blowing on their hands for a little warmth. Dry grass crackled underfoot. We were all hoping for an early spring. Winter was never easy at

San Carlos, and this had been no exception.

Upon arriving at Geronimo's wickiup, I coughed loudly in hope those within would acknowledge my presence. It wasn't our way to barge into another person's home without invitation. I waited patiently. The only sound from within was a series of grunts and squeals of delight. Geronimo, rutting with one of his younger wives.

Another sound attracted my attention. She, the lovely one, had just emerged from the next hut with a water jug in hand. After a quick smile, she lowered her head and set off for the stream. As I watched, the older woman came out and gave me a sour glance which made me avert my gaze from the sweetly swaying rump of the departing younger one.

"The old lady would cut your heart out if she knew what you were thinking," Geronimo said as he stooped and came out to stand beside me. I could only blush.

For a good twenty years or more—from the time the Mexicans killed his family and set him on a path of vengeance until John Clum brought him in without firing a shot—Geronimo had been the scourge of the West.

Yet, for those seeing him for the first time, Geronimo presented an unimpressive aspect. There was little at first glance to separate him from the average *indio*. His round face, framed by a mop of dark hair just starting to show traces of gray, was sun-ravaged and stern of expression. His dark gimlet eyes were like those of a sidewinder, and his mouth a wide slash, turned down at the edges.

Spend a minute in his presence, though, and you'd realize power radiated from this man like heat from a stove. You'd need to step back to keep it from burning you.

"What do you want, Mickey Free?" he asked.

I hesitated, seeking the right way to broach Sieber's question. Like most White Eyes, Al thought Geronimo would answer my questions just because we were both Apache. He didn't understand Geronimo was Bedonkohe, and I was raised Coyoteros, what the White Eyes call a White Mountain Apache. Our peoples have been allies and enemies at various times. And, Geronimo knew my background.

Sieber did, too, though maybe he'd forgotten. Not only was I a scout who'd assisted the Americans in making trouble for Geronimo and his people, I was also a half-breed. We were not enemies. Nor were we friends—despite the fact I'd now saved his life for a second time.

Geronimo stared at me with all the friendliness of a rattler. I noticed he'd aged in the months he'd spent at San Carlos. The skin stretched taut over his wide face was scoured with wrinkles, his hair was shot with gray, his broad shoulders were stooped, and there was a dimness in his dark eyes. San Carlos was hard on people. So it had been since the winter of 1875 when Al brought the Yavapai and Tonto here. The clans brought in later had fared no better. Many people had died, and Sieber had not been forgiven.

The shooting started before I had a chance to speak.

Now, Geronimo awaited an answer to his original question.

Dee-zho-ne, the beautiful one, had returned and was tending the morning fire. She'd recently arrived in the camp and I hadn't learned her name, which was why I'd taken to calling her Beauty. My gaze kept straying in her direction, even as Geronimo glared at me. "Did you come to see me or her?" he growled.

Reddening, I gave him my attention. "There's rumor—"

"There are always rumors."

"Someone is plotting to kill the chiefs who oppose leaving the reservation. Sieber thinks..."

Geronimo chuckled. "He thinks I'm behind it? Tell him—somebody just shot at *me*."

****

"He's a liar," Al said.

"I don't know. Those bullets came mighty close."

"He set it up to fool you. I'll bet you a month's pay," Sieber argued. "He's behind the plot."

I didn't remind Al nobody but him knew I planned on talking to Geronimo this morning. "He says he's not planning on leaving. Bad as things are, at least the women and children have food in their bellies. His youngest wife is pregnant. I think somebody else is behind it."

"Who? Take off the blinders, Mickey. He's run off from reservations before. He just doesn't want to go alone this time. He wants as many soldiers as he can recruit. Once he has them in his pocket, he'll go. Just you wait and see."

"I don't know. He could have left with Poinsenay. He didn't go with Victorio or old Nana. I've heard him chastise his men when Juh's recruiters come up from Mexico. I wouldn't be surprised if it was Juh working things from behind the scene."

History's like an old mirror. Distorted, smudged and fly-speckled. It doesn't always reflect things as they are.

I'd never been one for doing much talking. Al was always telling me, "Mickey, people haint never gonna know what you think unless you tell them." And Geronimo, who wasn't a windbag himself, sometimes called me *Ne-chotay*, the quiet one. Well, it was easier for them to say what they thought. No one could ever deny Mr. Sieber was a white man, and everybody knew for certain Geronimo was a damned redskin.

But who would listen to you when you were a scrawny one-eyed, alcoholic, near-illiterate bastard whose momma was a greaser and whose pap was either an Irish gringo or a Coyotero Apache? People just weren't inclined to put much stock in your words under those circumstances. So, I generally figured why waste time trying to tell them what you think?

That's the way I'd always felt, and that's why I tried to mind my own business, keep my opinions to myself and tried to get along with people as best as I could. The practice has saved me from a lot of knocks on the head.

Despite his always urging me to speak my mind, Al just shook his head in response to my comment and told me to keep nosing around and find out what Geronimo was up to.

****

"Mickey doesn't think Geronimo is behind it," Sieber said.

John Clum looked at me with surprise. Like Al, he wasn't used to me expressing an opinion. And, like Al, Clum didn't trust Geronimo. "What makes you think that?" he asked. His blue eyes sparkled with curiosity.

I'd always liked this boyish-looking young man. He tried to treat the people fairly, treat us like human beings in comparison to most of the agents and military people we'd known in the past. My White Mountain people called him *Nantan Betunnikeyah*, meaning Boss With the High Forehead, referring to his receding hairline.

It wasn't his fault the place the government had given him for a reservation was so barren people said *Usen* had created it just to make us appreciate all the good places He'd made for the Apache to live in. It wasn't Clum's fault politicians and the Army stole money intended for the reservation and meddled in his management practices.

The generals hated him. He was only twenty-six when he captured Geronimo last spring without a shot being fired on either side. Geronimo expected Turkey Gobbler—his insulting name for Clum—to kill him. Instead, John brought Geronimo and about a hundred of his people to San Carlos.

Before answering John's question, I considered what I'd witnessed and heard in the camps, searching for the words to convince Clum and Al of the rightness of my argument.

"When you brought Geronimo in, you put him and some others in chains and locked them up in a little room. He expected there'd be a trial, and then you'd hang him. Instead, the soldiers came, unlocked the chains and left him and his men go and find their families in the camp. That surprised him."

Al chuckled. "It'd shock the bastard even more if he knew John *did* want to hang him, and it was the Army that freed him."

Clum glowered at him. It was a secret that had

gained John some credence among the Chiricahua. "That doesn't mean he's happy about being here."

"None of the people are happy about being stuck in this burnt-out place, John," I said. "But, from what I've seen, Geronimo is content to stay put—at least, for the time being. No one is chasing or harassing him. There's been sickness all winter, and there's been bad feelings and fights between some of the bands. But you've made sure the sick ones get the medicine that's available and the tribal police do try to keep order. There's food for the women and children and old ones.

"Geronimo spends his days drinking and gambling and telling stories with his cronies and his nights making love to his young wives. He may not want to stay here forever. But I don't think he's ready to run yet."

Like Al, John listened to my words, nodding in agreement now and again, and paid me the courtesy of hearing me out. But I could tell from their eyes, neither man believed I was right.

Chapter 2

Some nights, I liked to roam about the camp, listening in on conversations, seeing what kind of information I could pick up. Al thought it was a bad idea. He said one of these nights, I was sure to wind up with a knife between my ribs.

I was cautious. I had a pretty good idea who I could trust and who I couldn't. I didn't have a problem when I was among my own White Mountain people. It was when I wandered into the camps of the Chiricahua, the Tontos, the Chihenne and others I had to watch my back.

There was more alcohol in the camps than you'd imagine. Soldiers sold at exorbitant prices from their rations, or they'd let civilian whiskey sellers in for a cut of the profit. It was no secret I liked a drink, myself. But I'd learned the booze was a bad idea for me—especially in those dangerous times. If I was among people I trusted, I might take a sip now and then just to be sociable. I made a practice of not doing that in Geronimo's camp. It wasn't him I worried about so much as some of his men. I knew his brothers Perico and Fun didn't like me. But they were brave and honorable men. Not the kind to stab another in the back. Chato, though, him or some of the wild young men who emulate him, I wouldn't turn my back on them.

I was making my way back to my quarters the night after my conversation with John Clum and Al when I became aware of someone coming up behind me. I ducked into the shadows between two wickiups. There was only a quarter-moon this night, but it shed enough light for me to recognize the slim figure who approached a moment later. I stepped out into her path.

"*Dagut'ee*," I greeted her. "What are you doing out here?"

The pretty one froze in her tracks. "I-I'm going home."

"You shouldn't be walking around by yourself at night. It's a dangerous thing for a young girl to do."

Her gaze averting mine, she said, "I had to deliver a message for my uncle."

"Does he often put you in danger?"

She met my stare boldly, now. "He wouldn't do that."

I needed to have a word with this man who put her at risk. "What's your uncle's name? Is he the one you live with?"

She stared at me a moment without answering. I could tell I'd frightened her. I wasn't sure if she'd recognized me. Many of the people feared us scouts as much as they did the tribal police. She might have known I was a scout, or just been scared of a man who stepped out of the dark to confront her. Her voice quavered when she told me, "He's not here. I stay with his parents."

Though she spoke Apache, there was something

foreign in her accent. "You're not Chiricahua are you?"

She shook her head. "Yavapai."

I longed to ask more about her history, but the sound of voices interrupted. Knowing one of the nearby wickiups had been abandoned, its former occupants having run away, I seized the girl's arm and ducked inside, hoping I'd chosen the right one. She resisted, thinking I had something else in mind. Clamping a hand over her mouth, I bade her be quiet, whispering that I meant her no harm. I felt her tense, but she complied, and we knelt side by side in the dark of the empty wickiup.

The hut held a residue of stale body odor, moldering vegetation and dust. Aside from these smells, I became conscious of the girl's respiration, the nervous quivering of her body, and her pleasant scent, like sweet sage. I longed to put an arm around her and quell her fear. Instead, I contented myself with the pleasure of sensing the warmth of her knee against mine.

Outside, I heard the slither of moccasins over hard-packed sand and the voices became louder. Two men. They paused in front of the wickiup. I recognized one voice, but not the other. "He says it's the only way," the familiar one said.

"I know, I know. I just don't like the idea. The old one has been good to our people. It makes me sad that he must die."

"Would you rather your family stay in this shithole?"

"Of course not. The sickness almost took my little

one. You know that. Stay here, and we'll all die. I'm with you. So are my brothers. Who will kill him?"

"We'll draw lots."

The two moved on now, their voices growing fainter as they walked away.

I nibbled my lower lip, wishing I'd been able to hear all of the conversation. Who did they plan to murder? And when?

The girl stirred beside me. I felt the soft touch of her hand on my wrist. "Those men—they're going to kill someone."

"That's what they said."

"But you must stop them. Maybe they will try to kill Goyathlay again," she said, using Geronimo's Bedonkohe name. "You must stop them. You saved him that other time."

"I'll do what I can," I told her, not sure if the assassins meant him or another. I was a little pleased she recognized me. "But first," I added, drawing her up, "we must get you safely home."

Occupied with our separate thoughts, neither of us spoke as we walked, and too soon, we'd reached her destination. "Thank you for bringing me home," she said, once more laying warm fingers on my wrist, before running off.

I watched her duck into the shelter of the wickiup, realizing I'd forgotten again to ask her name.

****

Sleep didn't come easy that night. I kept hearing that conversation over and over again in my head. The voice I'd recognized belonged to Chato, one of

Geronimo's close allies, and I couldn't help wondering if Al and Clum weren't right, after all. Could Geronimo be behind the plot and the attempt on his life just a ruse to draw attention away from him?

Still, I couldn't shake the idea I'd seen a hint of fear in his eyes yesterday morning as he'd glanced toward the bluff where the shots came from. Geronimo had proven his bravery time and again, but only a fool would deny being shaken at the thought of a close call with destiny. And Geronimo was no fool.

If not him, then who was stirring up the trouble...and who was the old one the plotters referred to? Could Chato be behind it? He was an arrogant, angry man, a fierce warrior in battle and respected by many. Yet, his bad temper marred his leadership ability. I couldn't see a majority of men acting on his behalf. He could be a ringleader, but I suspected someone else must be the instigator.

When my thoughts weren't focused on murder, they were on the girl. She'd haunted my thoughts day and night since the first time I'd seen her. That had been a week ago when she'd stood in line with other women as the contractors doled out promised rations, the usual allotments of wormy flour, lumpy sugar and maggot-infested beef.

Dee-zho-ne had stood out like a flower among those other worn-down and weary women. I couldn't keep my eyes off her, and I'd followed like a sick puppy as she lugged her burden back to camp, feasting my vision on her beauty like a bee drawn by sweet nectar. My original intent had been to offer to relieve her of the load, but I was too bashful and tongue-tied to speak.

There were other questions I had about her now. What had become of her parents? Who was this uncle that had her delivering messages late at night? What kind of message must it be that it couldn't be transferred in the daytime when it would be safer for the girl? Since she was Yavapai, I suspected the uncle might have been one of those brought to San Carlos in '75. Many of those people had fled in the wake of rumors the soldiers planned to butcher them.

Now, we were dealing with another round of rumors.

There was no end to trouble at San Carlos.

****

When dawn broke, I felt like I'd only slept minutes. More time than usual passed before I finally rose, dressed and went outside to greet the morning.

Though I hadn't had a sip of *tizwin* or any other alcohol, my headache seemed as bad as any resulting from a hangover. After relieving myself, I determined I needed a cup of strong coffee before seeing what duties Al had for me.

I'd also decided to do some more investigating before telling Sieber or anyone else about the conversation I'd overheard, and the suspicions it aroused.

****

I've been with Al Sieber since 1872, and though he's only a few years older than me, the man is like another father to me. That doesn't mean we always agree on things. Like any father and son, we have our disagreements.

But I can't think of many men I admire more.

Al served with the Union at Antietam, Gettysburg, and some other places I never heard of, and got some wounds which still plague him today. He came West after the war and hooked up with General Crook as chief of scouts in 1871. My brother Rope and me signed on with him soon after, and I became a sergeant the next year.

We were with Crook throughout the Tonto campaign and, let me tell you, those were some tough times. Lots of blood was spilled on both sides. But, thanks to the general, we got the Tonto and the Yavapai settled on the Verde. The people were doing well and were happy there until the damned politicians interfered and they had to be moved here to San Carlos. People just don't seem to understand it's the greed of those Indian agents and their backers that's usually the root of trouble on the reservations.

Those same civilians don't understand why my White Mountain people were willing to work as scouts and fight other Apache. As I said before, we've been friends with the Chiricahua, and also, we've feuded with them. In my own case, it was the Pinal who kidnapped me as a boy, but it was Cochise and his Chiricahua got the blame. I'm not happy about being responsible for a war between Cochise and the White Eyes. That war wasn't necessary, and I've carried a lot of guilt over all the people who lost their lives because of me.

When Nayundiie adopted me, I became a White Mountain Apache. I don't fight other Apache because

I might have some gringo blood. I fight because my White Mountain people want to live in peace—and the only way to get it is to put down those rebels who stir up trouble and can't seem to get it through their thick heads the White Eyes have the advantage, both in numbers and weapons. Like Chal-lipun, the great Yavapai leader, said when he surrendered, the White Eyes have too many cartridges of copper.

It's a sad fact, but until the Chiricahua and their allies finally lay down their guns there's going to be more bloodshed.

Chapter 3

A group of men were gathered around a bonfire which cast an orange light over their features. Standing back in the shadows, I studied their faces. At night, dressed as a warrior, I could move freely among those who didn't recognize me as a scout. I had to be more cautious when it came to those who did know me.

The only one of the men around the fire familiar to me was a Chihenne called Cuchillo, Spanish for *knife*. We had drank and gambled together in the past, and he mistakenly believed me to be a Chiricahua.

These men were drinking *tizwin* and playing the moccasin game. This is a popular guessing game played by many tribes. An object is hidden in one of a number of moccasins and the players wager on its location. Like many games, this has a religious origin. But nowadays, it's often just another excuse for gambling.

As I watched, these men drank and laughed, drank more and grew louder and more reckless in their wagering. *Tizwin* is a beer brewed from corn and isn't as strong as whiskey, but we are not a people good at drinking. Getting drunk is easy for some of us, and that can make a man dangerous—your brother one moment, and an enemy eager to slit your throat the next.

One of the players soon lost all he had to wager. He drew himself erect, gave a grunt of disgust, waved a hand at the others and staggered off into the darkness.

"Why are you standing back there in the dark?" Cuchillo asked, turning his head in my direction. "Come and join us. Have a drink. We need another player. Don't hide back there like a shy female."

It didn't surprise me. The man was as sharp as his name implied. He'd probably been aware of me the whole time I'd been watching them. I had no choice but to take the angry man's place. As I settled in between two men I didn't know, Cuchillo scooped up a handful of sunflower seeds and stuffed them in his mouth. Chomping on the seeds, he handed me a pot of beer. Then, he shook out the counting sticks, the signal for someone to make a wager.

Despite my desire not to drink, the beer tasted good going down. If I'd refused to drink, or to play, it would have aroused the suspicion of these men and put me in danger. That wasn't a risk I could take. So I quaffed another swallow before passing the jug to the man seated on my right.

"Where have you been?" Cuchillo asked, spraying seed shells from his mouth with his words. "Haven't seen you around for some time." He laughed. "Didn't run off, did you?"

I restricted my response to a grunt the men could interpret however they chose.

"We should all do that," the man to my left said. He

was an older fellow with a deep scar across one cheek. "All we do here is drink and gamble and get weak."

There came a couple of "Hu! Hu!" in agreement with his comment.

But another man glanced round nervously. "Better not be talking that way," he said. "There are spies everywhere."

"Ah, you talk like a woman, Taces," Cuchillo said, shaking a finger in the man's face. "What are you afraid of? Even Turkey Gobbler knows we all want to run away. It's just a question of when."

Scarface nodded. "The opportunity may come sooner than some think."

The fire crackled as sticks burned through and a showers of sparks rose amidst the dark smoke. Off in the distance, someone thumped on a drum and sang along in a hoarse voice.

"What do you mean?" I asked.

He peered at me with narrowed eyes. "I don't know you. You might be one of those spies Taces was talking about."

"He's not," Cuchillo vouched for me. "I've drunk with this man many a time. He looks a bit like the White Eyes, but he's a good Chiricahua. You can take my word for it. You can trust him."

His friends studied me, none of them saying more for the moment. My one blue-green eye and auburn hair I inherited from my father—whoever he might have been—had got me in trouble in the past. But the Apache have adopted lots of stolen white children over the years, and some of them have become more

Indian than those born red.

"He doesn't *look* like a Chiricahua," one of the men said.

"But I've killed enough Mexicans and Americans to prove I am one."

"Hu!" Cuchillo barked. "Let him be. Let's get back to the game."

"I'm more interested in what he was talking about," another man said, pointing at Scarface, for I soon learned this was the name they knew him by.

Scarface should have been wary of talking in front of strangers, but the alcohol had loosened his tongue and made him eager to brag. "We have a plan. Wait and see...soon, *many* people will be running off."

"What plan?" someone asked.

Scarface puffed up. Drawing himself erect, he exhibited a knowing smirk. "There are chiefs who are content to stay here. They want our people to rot and sit here like puppets of the White Eye." He waved a hand at the dark around our circle. "But there is a *real* leader out there. A man who wants to make us warriors again."

"How can it be?" the man called Taces asked. "The White Eyes are too strong. If we run, they hunt us down and bring us back."

"Not if we all go and scatter like seeds in the wind."

"Too many of our people listen to those chiefs you mentioned," I put in.

Scarface peered at me, his eyes glittering in the firelight. Then he said, "That's why those chiefs must die."

"You plan on killing them?"

He nodded. "We must."

"I heard someone tried to kill Geronimo yesterday," one of the men said.

"I heard that, too," Cuchillo said. "They say a scout saved him."

"Damned scouts. We should kill all of them, too."

"Geronimo is a great leader," I said. "This killing of the betrayers, it sounds like something he would do."

"Hah! He has grown soft in his old age. All he wants to do is drink whiskey and fuck his wives. Killing him would be an example to the others who want to stay here and behave like slaves."

"Maybe this man is right," Taces said, jerking his chin in my direction. "What if Geronimo had someone shoot at him just to fool the white eyes? It would not surprise me if he did that. He is a smart man."

I gave Taces an approving glance, happy he'd introduced the idea and I didn't have to broach it. But Scarface shot it down a moment later.

"Geronimo is not the leader he used to be. He has become an old woman. Our leader is a real man. He is—"

"Enough!"

We all turned our gaze on another man who'd sat silent throughout the conversation. He was a tall man, for an Apache, and wore a slouch hat that shadowed his face. But his eyes burned like hot coals as they scoured us now. "You talk too much," he chastised Scarface. His voice seemed familiar, though I couldn't place where I'd heard it before. "Taces has said there may be spies among us. I doubt this. You all seem like honorable men. But it is not wise to serve all your beans when you have no idea if there will be enough to eat tomorrow. It is better we stop this talk, play our game, and enjoy our beer."

We all hung our heads in shame, acknowledging his wisdom.

"Yes," Cuchillo said. "Let's have more beer."

****

I hadn't planned on staying as long or getting as drunk as I did. Good intentions were meaningless unless followed through.

When I finally parted from the others, my walk was unsteady, my pockets were empty of money, my head pounded, and I knew the sun would be rising soon after I collapsed onto my bed. Bad enough I'd given into the attraction of alcohol, I'd also gambled away my last centavo—and pay day was still many days off.

But I had gathered some information that might not have been available otherwise.

A voice hailed me as I stumbled off through the dark. Warily, I turned to confront the person hurrying up to me. *Scarface. What does he want?*

"Did you mean what you said?" he asked, sidling up to me.

What had I said? Had alcohol loosened my tongue more than intended? "What do you mean?"

He raised a hand, seeking a moment to recover his wind. He breathed heavily and his face seemed dark with exertion in the dim light offered by the moon. "You walk fast," he said when able to speak again. "I didn't know which direction you'd gone. I had to run to find you." He bent over, placing his hands on his knees and gulping in cool air. "Not good for an old man."

"Why'd you want to catch me? I have no more money."

"Not your money I want," he said, straightening up and giving me a tight grin. "You seemed interested in my words back there."

I nodded, cautious. "What you said makes sense. We need to get our people away from this evil place."

He peered at me. "Cuchillo says we can trust you."

"Who's *we*?"

He waved a hand again. "Never mind that for now. Can we trust you?"

I stared back at him. "As much as I trust you."

This time, he nodded. "Do you wish to learn more of our plans?"

"I would."

"Then meet me tomorrow. I will tell you a place."

****

There are times when you know you've made a mistake and it's too late to turn it around. This might prove to have been one of those. I could have blamed the *tizwin*, being over-tired, or a dozen other things. But I knew the real source was none of those. It was my damnable curiosity.

I'd convinced myself Geronimo wasn't behind the plot and it was up to me to prove it to Al and Clum. Even if it meant losing my own scalp in the process.

A chorus of grunts, snores and farts greeted me as I stumbled into our quarters. Like the soldiers, we scouts were housed in barracks rather than being left to erect our own wickiups. Some of the men complained and said they'd rather we were left to our native traditions. I'd got used to having a real roof overhead and a bed to sleep on, though some of my *compadres* continued to bunk on the floor. I stepped on one of them and he unleashed a torrent of swear words in Apache, Spanish and broken English.

I ignored him and collapsed on my bed.

Chapter 4

"You're gonna get yourself killed," Al said when I told him about my evening adventure.

"That's not my intention."

"You plan on meetin' this guy?"

"That's the idea."

He brushed a hand across his sandy hair and scowled at me with his dark eyes. "Maybe these renegades didn't recognize you, but a lot of Geronimo's henchman know exactly who you are. What are you gonna do when you run into one of them?" When he gets agitated his German accent becomes more pronounced, and sometimes the way a word comes out, it makes me grin. I wasn't grinning now.

I didn't think it would be in my best interest to mock him. Nor did I think it wise to mention Chato just yet. "Like I told you before, I don't think Geronimo's involved in this."

"I think you're being naïve, Mickey. Your buddy Geronimo ain't no saint, and he ain't dumb. You think some other gang could be plottin' trouble and him not be aware of it?"

I gritted my teeth and didn't say it, but I knew what I'd seen in Geronimo's eyes that other morning. It seemed clear to me—Geronimo hadn't asked someone to take a shot at him, especially not one that came as close as it did.

Al tugged on his mustache and spat tobacco juice into a can. "This guy you called Scarface," he continued, "he wants you to meet him off the rez?"

I nodded.

"See. That's why it sounds like a trap to me. Him and his cronies get you out there alone, what makes you think they're not gonna take your hair?" He plucked the wad of tobacco from his mouth and disposed of it in the can.

"It's a chance I got to take. I've got to convince him to trust me."

"But why not have this meeting on the reservation?"

"Him and the others complained of spies being all around. I don't think they were talking about just us. Even if they don't agree with them, there are people who wouldn't cotton to the idea of murdering some of the old chiefs. Scarface and Cuchillo were hesitant about saying too much in front of the bunch we were with last night. And there was another guy who kept in the shadows so I couldn't see his face. He seemed to be in charge, and he chastised them for talking in front of strangers."

"You didn't recognize him?"

"Like I said, he kept to the shadows and had a hat pulled down over his face."

"Well, it seems like no matter what I say you're gonna go off and meet with this scar-faced fellow."

"I am. I think I must."

"Damn, Mickey." Al's brow furrowed and he gave

me a look I could only interpret as one of affection—
though he'd be the last to admit feeling such an emo-
tion for any other human being. "You're one of my
best scouts and translators. I don't wanna lose you.
I'm not gonna let you go out there alone. You take—"

"I can't bring somebody else. He said to come
alone. How am I gonna get him to trust me if I don't
do as he said?"

"Gimme a chance to finish my sentence before you
go interrupting me, dang it. I wasn't talkin' about
sending nobody with you. I was gonna say, take care
to lay down a trail so's Rope can follow you and save
your worthless ass if they do try to kill you."

I smiled. Al knew my foster brother *Tlodilhil*, called
John Rope by the White Eyes, was the only one of my
fellow scouts I fully trusted. We'd done a good part of
our growing up under the tutelage of his father
Nayundiie. We rode in on the same pony to sign on as
scouts, and we've been just as close ever since.

****

Our rendezvous was in a ravine in the hills overlooking the reservation. The Gila Mountains were a
hazy purple barrier to the north. Clum's policy grant-
ed the Apache a certain amount of freedom to move
around. I guess originally he hoped hunting would
supplement the meager food allotments provided by
the government, but there were too many people
crowded together, and it didn't take long for game to
become scarce. Sometimes men did still go into the
hills, hoping to scare up a rabbit or some quail, and
the soldiers didn't try to stop us if we went out alone

or in groups of two or three.

There wasn't much cover, the rough ground covered mostly in cactus or yucca as I rode uphill, and I worried the renegades might spot Rope if he got in too close. I had to trust they'd take him for a hunter if they did see him.

Despite my bravado in speaking to Al, I had to admit going into this nest of men I didn't really know made me nervous.

Descending into the canyon, I smelled smoke and it wasn't long before I came upon Scarface and Cuchillo sitting by a small fire. A fringe of trees along the top screened their camp from the view of anyone above. Cuchillo waved to me and indicated I should tether my horse in the shade of a couple of stunted cottonwoods where they'd left their mounts.

They were munching dried agave and washing it down with coffee brewed in a blue enamel pot leaning on the coals. Cuchillo handed me a slice of the fruit when I squatted next to him. "Told you he'd come," he said to the older man.

"I had no doubt," Scarface said, grinning at me.

I chewed the tasty morsel, waiting for him to make the first move.

He drained his cup and held it out for Cuchillo to refill. Only after he'd taken a swallow did he speak. "You agree, our people will die if they stay at San Carlos?"

I nodded. "I do."

"But if we leave in small bands, the Army will just hunt us down and bring us back."

Another nod of agreement.

"We must *all* leave. Then, we will be strong enough to fight the Army and they will fear coming after us."

Considering the various bands housed at San Carlos and the antipathy between them I didn't think it very likely they'd all agree to leave together. But I didn't mention my disbelief. "How do we accomplish that?" I asked. "Many of our leaders say we must stay, or the Army will wipe us out."

"Traitors!" he snapped. "We must silence the voices of these old men and convince the people we are right. It has been decided, the only way is to kill those who speak against leaving."

"Kill these respected men?" I gave him a shocked look, as though the thought had never occurred to me.

"They are no longer *worthy* of respect," Cuchillo said, his words distorted as he masticated the tough fruit. He raised a hand and brought it down in an arc. "We must cut ourselves off from them."

Scarface peered at me, his dark eyes scanning for any sigh of revulsion. "Are you agreed?" he asked, finally.

"We must do what is necessary for the *Ndee*," I told him, using our name for the People.

"Good. That's what I hoped to hear. Because my brother Cuchillo trusts you, I will trust you. The Prophet is not so easily convinced, though. He says you must be tested before you hear more."

"The Prophet? Who's that?"

"If you pass the test, perhaps you will meet him."

"What kind of test?"

"You will be given the name of a man who you

must kill. When that is done, you will learn more."

"You want me to kill somebody?"

He shook his head. "It is not my decision. It is just how it must be."

I decided I must take a chance. "Is Geronimo the Prophet?"

Cuchillo laughed, spraying coffee from his mouth. "He Who Yawns is not a prophet. He has become an old woman. I told you that last night. Or did the *tizwin* dim your memory?"

"Enough," Scarface growled, glaring at him.

"I heard someone shot at Geronimo," I said. "Is he one of the leaders to be killed?"

"The man who took that shot failed his test. You do not want to make his mistake."

"I don't want to make any mistakes."

"That is good to hear. Go now. You will be contacted and given a name. When the time comes, do not fail your test."

****

I met up with Rope back at camp.

"Your new friends must have their ears stuffed with wool stolen from Navajo sheep," he said with a grin. "I laid up in the grass so close to you I feared they might hear my breathing. Did you know I was there?"

Rope was short and stocky, but tough as a cholla cactus. There was no other man I'd prefer to have my back in a tight spot. "No," I told him, knowing it was what he hoped to hear. *Tlodilhil* is proud of his stalking skills. Truth is, I hadn't heard him either. I could have told him so, but that would only have made him more boastful. So, instead, I asked, "Could you hear what was said?"

"Every word—well, except for what Cuchillo mumbled with his mouth stuffed full of agave. So, who do you think they want you to kill?"

"I don't know. The other night I overheard two men talking about killing one of the old chiefs. They didn't mention a name, though. I hope they don't ask me to kill one of the old ones I like."

Rope looked aghast. "You're not really going to go through with it, are you?"

"We need to find out who this 'Prophet' is."

"Sure. But there must be another way. Not murder."

I agreed with my brother. I didn't want to kill some innocent old man. Still, I was anxious to see who they wanted out of the way.

"One of the men I overheard that night was Chato."

Rope wrinkled his brow. "Surely you don't think he's this 'Prophet'?"

"Of course not. That hothead doesn't have the makings of a leader. But he is involved."

"Shall we go and tell Sieber what you found out?" Rope asked as we unsaddled our mounts, wiped them down and rewarded them with some fodder before turning them out in the corral.

"Let's hold off on that for a while. I think I might go and see if anyone else has shot at Geronimo today."

Rope chuckled. "You don't have to lie to me, big brother. I know you're not interested in Geronimo's health. This is just an excuse to go gawk at the pretty one who lives next to his wickiup."

"Do you blame me?"

He punched me on the shoulder. "Of course not. I have seen her. She is certainly worth a man's attention. Perhaps I should come with you. I like looking at beautiful women, too."

Chapter 5

This wasn't to be a day for gawking at Dee-zho-ne, though.

We encountered Al as we walked back to the barracks from the corral and, before he'd said a word, we'd both noticed the worried look clouding his weathered face.

"Something wrong, sir?" Rope asked.

"Yeah," he said in a strained voice. "There's been a shooting."

Geronimo. Had someone else made good on the test?

"Where?" Rope asked.

I followed up with "Who?" before Sieber had a chance to reply.

"In the Tonto camp. Don't know who yet. I'm on my way over there now."

"We'll go with you," I told him.

"Uh-uh," Al muttered, shaking his head. "Rope can go with me. If you're gonna play this game of yours, you don't wanna be seen with us. You can wander in to satisfy your curiosity. But stay in the background and steer clear of our company."

I had to agree, what he said made sense.

It occurred to me I hadn't worn my uniform in several days. Wearing a faded cotton shirt, breechclout, leggings and moccasins and with a scarlet headband, I looked little different than other *indios*—unless I came across someone who recognized me as a scout. I figured there would be a crowd. Trouble always drew people like flies to a rotting carcass. If my luck held out, I'd be able to blend in with the other spectators.

****

A sullen crowd surrounded the murder scene, so many people Sieber, Rope and the soldiers accompanying them had a hard time getting through for a peek at the victim. The soldiers had to shove people aside, and they weren't gentle about it.

Looking over the shoulders of others in front of us, I asked the man next to me, "What happened?"

"I just got here," he replied. "They say somebody got killed."

A broad-shouldered man with a crooked nose turned to confront us. "Hawk's Brother," he said. "They say the old man got up during the night and came outside to take a piss. Somebody slit his throat." He spat off to the side. "It isn't even safe to come out to take a piss at night in this damned place."

"Why would they do that?" I asked.

"Maybe he was messing with someone else's woman," my neighbor said.

"He was an old man," our informant said. "Too old to do any more than look at a woman. No. It had nothing to do with women."

"Some are saying it was because he advised our

people not to run away," another man offered.

"That could be true," a man behind us added. "He has told us, even if the food and other things are bad in this place, things would be worse if we tried to leave. The soldiers would kill us, rape our women and eat our children."

"Another man came and talked to us one night," our informant said. "He said if all the people came together as one clan and ran away to the mountains together, the *Ga'an* would protect us."

"I have heard of this man," someone said. "He spoke to the Mimbreno, too."

"You know this man?" I asked our informant.

He stared at me, suspiciously. "Why?"

"Just curious."

"Maybe this one wants to run away, too," my neighbor said and chuckled.

"Who doesn't?" I said with a shrug.

"Hu! Hu!"

Crooked nose grunted in agreement. "I did not know this man. By his accent, I thought he might be Chihenne, but I wasn't sure. He was only here one time. Besides, he wore a mask."

This was an interesting detail. If a man had to hide his identity from those he chose to entice it might indicate a vulnerability we could exploit. I asked if anyone knew who he was. If they did, they weren't talking. I had more digging to do.

Sieber, Rope and the soldiers had gathered what information they could about the murder and were preparing to leave. The mourning family would be allowed access to the body, now, and could begin burial ceremonies. The keening began immediately, and I grimaced at the thought of all the people who have suffered since coming to this cursed place.

In the past, the body would have been carried into the mountains and concealed in a cave, its whereabouts a secret to all save those who brought it to this place. It must be done quickly, or ghosts would bring more misfortune in their wake. Nowadays, the Army does not often permit this practice, insisting the dead be buried in a cemetery on the reservation. This might be why there was so much talk of ghosts in the camps, even among those who didn't believe in them before.

I felt sorry for this old man I'd never met—and for his family. I did not think it right they should suffer because others wanted the people to run away.

Curiosity satisfied, the crowd began to drift away. Soon, only the old man's family would be alone with their sorrow. With a final compassionate glance in their direction, I turned to head back to the barracks. A chill ran up my spine as I felt someone's eyes on me.

Cuchillo grinned and raised a hand in greeting as I spun round. Behind him, in the departing crowd, I spied the back of a tall man wearing a slouch hat, and I shivered again.

****

"So you didn't recognize this tall fellow?" Rope asked later as we ate lunch.

"I still haven't seen his face."

"You think he might be this *Prophet* they talk

about?"

"Dunno," I told him, sopping up the last of my beans with a heel of bread. "He could be. Then again, he could be just another follower."

"But you said he seems to have some power over the others."

"He does. Hopefully, when Scarface contacts me again, I'll find out more."

Rope peered at me for a long moment. Then he said, "Al is right, you need to be careful, my brother. This hole you are digging is getting deeper, and you may have trouble climbing out. What are you going to do when they give you the name of the man you're to kill?"

It wasn't a question I had an answer for. I shrugged. "I'll think of something when the time comes."

When we came outside, we found two other scouts sitting on the steps of the building. Dutchy looked up with a glum expression but didn't greet us. The other man, whose name was Crow, didn't even bother to look up.

"What's with you two?" Rope asked.

"A bad thing has happened," Dutchy said. "Crow's nephew killed himself."

Given the state of despondency on the reservation, news of a suicide wouldn't normally have been a surprise. But I knew Crow's mother had been a Chiricahua and, despite his being a scout, he maintained close ties with them. "I'm sorry to hear this," I told him. "Do you know what happened?"

Crow was older than Rope and me, and by his experience and valor had earned the respect of all the scouts. He raised his head and gazed up at me now and I was struck by how much older he looked, though I couldn't be sure if it were the result of his sorrow, or that I just hadn't noticed before. His hair was streaked with gray, his eyes were dim and sunk in deep hollows, and the creases in his flesh were like ravines.

"The boy was keeping bad company," Crow said. "His mother asked me to talk to him, and I did. He got angry and refused to hear my words. I thought I'd give him time and he would come around." He eyes glistened in the light. Then, he added, "Instead, he went out in the hills and hanged himself. His little brother found him this morning."

Rope and I exchanged a glance. It was a very bad thing for children to see a dead person. But I also thought about the warrior who had failed to kill Geronimo. It made sense he would have been a Chiricahua.

"We are sorry for your loss," my brother told Crow.

"These bad people you spoke of—do you know who they are?"

He shook his head. "No. Only that his mother said they were giving him bad ideas—making him talk about running away from San Carlos."

"Something many want to do," Rope offered.

"Yes. But that wasn't all of it. He blamed Geronimo for keeping the people here. I told him Geronimo is a great leader and deserved his respect. He said his friends believe Geronimo has turned into an old woman." He shook his head. "It is a sad thing when the young turn on their elders. And now, he has shamed his family."

I wondered—had the young man killed himself...or, had he had help?

****

Drums and singing greeted me as I stalked into Geronimo's camp later in the evening. A gibbous moon floated past wispy clouds in a dark sky and there was a nip in the air. But, as I drew nearer, it became obvious the dancers didn't mind the chill.

It was a social dance, and it gladdened me to see smiles on the faces of the boys as they circled round the girls in the middle row who also grinned shyly as they lowered their eyes and shuffled round and round under the lustful gaze of their lovers.

Geronimo sat with the musicians, tapping a curved stick on a drum, his eyes closed as he sang, his song making the boys laugh and causing the girls to bashfully look at the ground. Geronimo had a good, warm voice, and he knew the funny songs as well as the sacred ones. He sang:

Young woman, you are thinking of something;
Young woman, you are thinking of something,
You are thinking of what you are going to get:
That man of whom you are thinking is worthless.

We all laughed at his words, knowing it was common for a girl to expect a gift from the man on whom she has cast her eyes and feelings. His song spoke of the disappointment she would experience.

I stood watching, lost in my own thoughts as one dance finished and another began to form. It was then someone touched me on the shoulder. I turned in time to see Dee-zho-ne tilt her head toward the dancers, and give me a shy smile. What else could I do? I followed, and stepped into line before her.

My heart thudded in my chest and my gaze was fixed on her like a bird captured by the stare of a snake. Of course, she was no snake. I just could not believe she might be attracted to a man as ugly as me, yet...I was the one she'd invited to join her in the circle.

She was so lovely. I couldn't believe my luck. Unlike the calico camp dresses some of our women have taken to wearing, my dance partner wore a traditional fringed buckskin dress. Circular holes in the cape were backed with scarlet color and there were tin cone jinglers hanging from the fringe and on the edges of her skirt which played their own music with her movements. Her copper skin glistened in the firelight and her dark eyes flashed in those rare times they met mine.

As the dance ended and we broke formation, my fingers chanced to brush against the soft flesh of her hand and I jolted it away as though stung. It was a sting I would have eagerly sought again, though she didn't seem to have noticed its effect on me.

As we walked she leaned forward and whispered into my ear, "Goyathlay warns you to be careful, Mickey Free." Then she melted into the crowd.

****

Stunned, I stood a moment, considering her words. *She knew who I was.* And, her message came from Geronimo. I was devastated. She hadn't picked me because she was attracted to me. She'd chosen me for the opportunity to deliver a message from Geronimo. What did this mean?

There were questions I needed to ask. I sought her in the gathering and couldn't find her. I went to her wickiup, but no one responded to my calls. Dee-zho-ne had disappeared like a ghost into the mist.

Chapter 6

"Damn it, Mickey," Al said, "I told you, you're playin' with fire. If this girl knows who you are and she's deliverin' messages for Geronimo, how many other people do you think you're foolin' into thinking you're a renegade?"

I had no answer and I hung my head to avoid Sieber's scrutiny. Was he right? Was Geronimo setting me up for betrayal? I still didn't think so. Despite what others might feel about him, Geronimo is one of the wisest men I've ever known and there isn't much goes on in this camp he isn't aware of. I truly believe his warning came in gratitude for me saving his life. Obviously, he'd heard something that put me in danger. Given his position, it wasn't like he could come right out and cozy up to a scout without losing face. That's why he went through the girl.

But that raised another question. If she knew who I was, could I trust her?

"It's time you get back to doin' the job you're paid for and stop this spy business," Al interrupted my thoughts.

"What do you mean?"

"Just what I said. I got a job for you. The agent over on the Salt claims some of our people have been stealin' cattle and mules from the Pima. He wants—"

"Sounds like a job for the tribal police, not us."

"They got enough right here. That's why I'm sending you and Tomas over to talk to him."

"Why Tomas? Why not me and Rope?" I don't have a thing against Tomas. The White Eyes call him Tommy. He's an older fellow, generally on the quiet side, and probably the calmest man I've ever met. Nothing seems to rattle him.

Al scowled at me and scratched at his rump. "I know you're not fond of the Pima. That's why I'm sending Tommy with you. He's less likely to lose his temper when one of those sod-busters starts accusing you of lusting after his sheep."

I saw there was no point then in arguing with Sieber. Like I said, I've nothing against Tomas. It's just—when ordered to do something I don't particularly like—I'd rather have the company of my brother than somebody whose manner I'm less familiar with.

****

It was more than sixty miles from San Carlos to the Salt River Reservation. Fortunately, we weren't going that far. Arrangements had been made for the agent, a man named Stockton, and a couple of tribal delegates to meet us where Cherry Creek flowed into the dry Salt. A short distance for us and a long journey for them. They must have been really fussed up to come all this distance to confront us.

We Apache had always despised the *O'otham*, as they call themselves, and they were one of our main targets in the old days when we raided for our living.

They were mostly farmers who didn't like to fight. But, I'd admit, when they got angry, they could become strong warriors. Another thing we didn't like about them was they never opposed the White Eyes and had grown rich by trading with the Americans who traveled across their lands headed for the gold fields in California.

I mused on these things as we rode along and it was only when I glanced at him I realized Tomas hadn't said two words to me since we'd saddled up and ridden out of camp. "What are you thinking about?" I asked.

Tomas was tall for an Apache, but broad-shouldered and strongly built for a man his age. His dark eyes seemed to never flinch. His long hair was streaked with gray and he wore no headband, so sometimes it fell across his face, putting it in shadow. Today, he wore a scarlet shirt and ragged trousers some soldier had given him. A copper gorget at his throat caught the sun and threw off beams of light.

He gazed at me for a long moment without comment. Then, he grinned, giving his face a less stern countenance. "I been thinking you would probably be happier back in the barracks with a pot of *tizwin*."

"Wouldn't you?"

"I'm glad to have something to do. This is better for a man than sitting around drinking and gambling."

I didn't know if he meant it as an insult or not. I didn't reply.

A few miles more down a dusty, sandy track and we came to the meeting place. The Pima and their envoy hadn't arrived yet. We dismounted and allowed our animals to forage on the coarse grass in a nearby slough. We hunkered side by side on a fallen log and Tomas lit a pipe.

It was a pleasant afternoon, the sun high but warm on our faces. The sweet odor of burning tobacco mingled with that of sun-warmed grass and earth. The sound of running water in the creek blended with the hungry chomping of the horses and the twitter of birds hidden in the brush.

A thought occurred to me then as we rested. "You're Yavapai, ain't you?"

Tomas turned his head slightly to peer at me. "I am."

"Maybe you can help me with something."

"If I can."

"How do you talk to a Yavapai woman—to test if she might like you?"

He grinned again, showing good teeth. "Are you thinking of offering ponies for one of our women?"

"I might be."

Before he could reply, we were interrupted by the arrival of Stockton and his Pima. The agent was a red-haired man with a full beard. The fellow was so corpulent I felt immediate pity for his poor horse. "Where's your agent?" he barked.

"Back in his office."

"I didn't ride all this way to talk to a couple of Indians," he said.

"That's what you got, though."

With a grunt, he slid off his horse and stretched, bracing his back with both hands.

The two Pima with him were sour-looking individuals, short, dark-skinned and dressed in cast-off White Eye clothes. The older of the two glowered at me, pursed his lips and said, "You bring money?" He was nearly as fat as Stockton.

"Why would I bring money?"

"To pay for cows."

"I don't have no cows—not yours or nobody else's."

"We were told the Army would pay for the stolen animals," Stockton said.

The other Indian dismounted and slapped his pony on the rump. It went off to join ours in grazing. The rider hitched up his britches and circled around behind us. I noticed a big knife sheathed at his side.

"Nobody told us about any payment," I told them. "We was just sent out to talk to you."

"No want talk," the older Pima said. "Just want money."

"Well, you're just plumb out of luck then. 'Cause we haint got none."

Stockton sidled up close to me, his piggy eyes flicking from me to Tomas and back again. There were food stains on his coat and the stench coming off him testified he hadn't had a bath in too long a time. He gestured with his chin at his companions. "They ain't gonna be happy about this," he said.

I shrugged. "Like I said, nobody mentioned money to us."

Stockton glanced up at the fat Indian. "Whadya think, Wawuk? You gonna take that for an answer?"

The man called Raccoon gave just the hint of a nod to his companion and I spun around just in time to see him draw that big knife and advance on Tomas.

Quick as a rattler, Tomas smashed the butt of his rifle into the face of his attacker. There was a pop of breaking bone and the Pima dropped in his tracks.

Catching the movement, I turn and saw Wawuk draw a rusty old Lindsay .44 from the folds of his clothing and point it at my chest. With a grin, he drew back the hammer and pulled the trigger. There was an audible click but, fortunately for me, the cap failed to ignite. Before he could attempt a second charge, I raised my Springfield and blew him out of the saddle. He plopped onto the ground with a thud like a fallen bale of hay.

Meanwhile, the agent had drawn a Colt which he pointed at my head.

Before he had a chance to fire, a hot burst of lead spun past me from behind, and Stockton's head exploded with a spray of blood.

"What the hell did you do that for?"

"You rather I let him shoot you?"

He had a point. "No. But what are we gonna do now? What do we tell Sieber?"

"Tell him what happened."

"The Pima, we might get away with. But you shot an agent."

"Who was going to shoot you. I had no choice." He stepped over to where his assailant lay groaning. Tomas pressed the barrel of his rifle to the man's temple and fired another shot. The sound echoed off along the stream like a clap of thunder.

****

Tomas was surprisingly talkative on the ride back

to San Carlos. Killing made most men glum. For others, it seemed to be an energizing factor, almost transforming them into another person. I'd never witnessed a killing by this scout before, but he seemed to be in the latter category. Rather than worrying about what we would report about the incident, he plied me with questions about the Yavapai maiden I'd mentioned earlier.

"Is she pretty?"

"More than pretty. She's beautiful." Despite my despair, I responded to his questions as if focusing on her might cleanse my spirit.

This prompted a bark of a laugh. "What's her name?"

"Truth be told, I don't know. Never got around to asking."

"You can't court a girl if you don't even know her name."

"I'm not sure I should be courting her."

"Why? You said she's beautiful."

"And she is. But I don't know if I can trust her."

Tomas gave me a curious look, his lips twisting into another semblance of a smile. "Why is that?"

"I caught her wandering around the camps one night. She told me she was delivering a message for her uncle."

"What kind of message?"

"She refused to say."

"Who is this uncle?"

"Don't know. She lives with his parents, but not in the Yavapai camp where they should be. They're over in the Bedonkohe camp. I figure the uncle might be a runaway, and intent on stirring up trouble."

He gazed at me with an unreadable expression on his face. "But you don't know that."

"No. Like I said, I don't know much about her. Only that her beauty draws me."

"Maybe that is enough, and maybe it is not. Maybe you are too suspicious, Mickey Free. Her uncle might be a good man, and his messages harmless."

"There's something else."

"Oh, what might that be?"

"The other night she brought me a message from Geronimo."

This put a different expression on his stern face. It was like a cloud changing a sunny day to a stormy outlook. "Why would a Yavapai woman deliver messages for that Chiricahua dog?"

Chapter 7

Al Sieber rubbed a big hand across his face. His gaze scanned Tomas and then came back to me. "Whadya do with the bodies?"

"Left them where they fell," Tomas said before I had a chance to answer. "We brought their horses with us."

Al scowled at him. "You brung their horses, but you left them layin' out there for the buzzards to feed on?"

"We had no wagon, Mr. Sieber. We figured we'd report what happened, then go back and bury them."

"We haint gonna bury them," Al growled in response. "The bodies got to be taken back to their people for proper burial. We can let the Army do that. But, Jesus, did you have to kill the agent, too? How am I gonna explain that?"

"We had no choice," Tomas told him. "They attacked us. The agent would have killed Mickey if I hadn't shot him."

I'd already expressed my appreciation several times to Tomas for saving my hide. But I still couldn't get my head around why we'd been attacked in the first place. I could accept that the Pima may have hated us enough to have their own reasons for attacking us.

It just didn't make sense Stockton had gone along with it. What could his motivation have been?

While I pondered this, Al had been musing on the overall situation. He poured a cup of coffee from the pot which stood always like a fixture atop the Acme Red Jacket stove in his little office. After a test swig to gauge its warmth, he carried the cup back to his desk and settled himself on his swivel chair. He took another moment to light a cigar, blew a swirl of smoke, and jabbed a finger at Tomas. "I'm gonna let you guide the soldiers back to where you left the carcasses. Mickey's gonna help me draft a report for them to carry back to Salt River. Come on back when you're ready to go and we'll go over and tell the Army what happened."

After Tomas left, I asked Al what he intended to say about Stockton.

Tapping his pen on the desktop, he said, "Only thing I *can* say—damned Pima killed him when they decided to attack you and Tommy. I sure as hell can't say my scouts killed a government man."

"Why do you think he was working with them?"

Al hunched his shoulders. "Must have been money in it someplace for him. That's the only explanation I can see. Never met the man, but I haint never met no honest agent yet—except for mebbe Clum."

It would be some time before we had a firm answer to the question of Stockton's involvement.

****

There were some who considered me a natural born killer. Truth was, I didn't like killing any more than anyone else, and I felt bad about shooting that Pima. Whether you believe that or not is up to you.

A lot of stories have sprouted up as a result of my history, and not the half of them is true.

It sure wasn't my idea to be kidnapped by those Pinal back in 1861 when my mama was living with the Irishman John Ward. I'm not happy about some of the things happened because of them taking me. It was Lieutenant George Bascom made the mistake of blaming Cochise and precipitating a bloody war that raged on for a decade. I was only thirteen or fourteen years old at the time, and there was nothing I could have done to prevent it.

Fortunately for me, Nayundiie decided to adopt me, and that's how I became Rope's brother. When the two of us joined up with Al Sieber he became like another father to us. And I sure don't regret the path he's led us on.

****

Given my despondency over what had happened with the _O'otham_ I wasn't looking for company that night. But company found me.

I'd bought a bottle of whiskey from one of those peddlers who are like cockroaches on the reservation. Fortified with the first few sips, I walked—bottle in hand—out across the scrublands, up a rise and into a mixed forest of oak and pine where I found myself a convenient seat on a stump affording a view out over the desert below.

There, surrounded by the good scent of pitch mingled with warm earth, I watched the sun go down and attempted to deaden my bad thoughts with the whiskey and the sounds of nature. It didn't work. The whiskey tasted vile, the sounds were the harsh scolding of a crow disturbed by my presence and my thoughts refused to abandon me. I corked the bottle and tossed it aside.

"Good thing there are lots of pine needles on the ground or it might have broke and wasted all that good tonic," a voice said from behind me.

Scarface came out of the shadows and squatted next to me.

"How did you find me?"

"I followed you. Do you always drink alone?"

I grunted.

Undeterred, he retrieved my bottle, drew out the cork and took a big swallow. "A man should never drink alone," he said, handing me the bottle and wiping his mouth on his shirt sleeve.

"Sometimes a man *wants* to be alone," I told him, accepting the bottle.

"If a man has troubles he should share his whiskey and seek the advice of a friend."

After taking a drink, I passed the bottle back to him. "Sometimes a man must work out his problems for himself."

"That depends. What kind of problem does my friend have tonight?"

I shrugged. "Maybe I am bothered by a woman's behavior," I said, not caring to reveal my actual concern.

Scarface laughed. "If your problem is a woman, then your friend can not help you. In all my years, I have not learned how to understand them." He paused for another drink, then asked, "Is she pretty, this one?"

"The most beautiful I have ever seen."

He laughed again. "Then you have real trouble, my friend. Beautiful women are always the most trouble." He handed me the bottle.

I couldn't disagree, and sought solace from the bottle.

"I have news of another kind," Scarface said, gesturing for return of the whiskey.

"Oh? What news?"

There was a different light in his dark eyes as he squinted at me. "Your target has been selected."

"And, who is it I'm to kill?"

"Geronimo."

****

"Well, I guess that puts him in the clear."

"Maybe," Al said, still not willing to relent on his suspicion. "You ever stop to think, *he* might be the one putting you to the test?"

"Pretty dangerous way of doing it," John Clum said. "No. I think Mickey might be right about this." He rose, went to the stove and refilled his coffee mug. "Somebody else is pullin' the strings on this one. I believe Geronimo has become a legitimate target for them."

Sieber shook his head. "I don't think so, John. I feel—"

"Hold on a second," Clum said, raising a hand. "Hear me out. Despite what you and I think of the man, Mickey is right—Geronimo is one smart fellow. He knows Mickey is a scout and not a renegade. He knows—"

"Exactly my point," Al interrupted. "He knows Mickey haint gonna shoot him. So, when Mickey fails their test, they have an excuse to kill *him*."

I didn't like the situation, either way. I didn't want to shoot Geronimo, and I didn't want to become a target for the renegades for not doing it. "What am I supposed to do?" I asked them. "Either way, I'm right square in the middle."

Both men stared at me as though I had no right to butt into their debate. "Well?" I asked. "What's your advice?"

A period of silence and more stares ended with Sieber commenting, "I suppose you'll just have to play it by ear."

Great advice. Since they offered no help for my dilemma I walked out of the office. Clouds rising like white rocks and a wind from the south that swirled dust devils across the plaza brought hope of some rain to come, though I feared the temperature might make it hail or snow, instead. Some soldiers stood down by the corral, watching a wrangler work the horses. A mule brayed and was answered by the nickering of a horse.

I plunked down on the steps, elbows planted on my knees and my chin propped in my hands, pondering what I might do. As I sat there mulling my situation, another movement across the plaza caught my attention. *Dee-zho-ne.*

What was she doing here? Except on allotment

days, people seldom strayed from their own camps on the reservation. I rose and hurried after her.

"What are you doing here?" I asked, seizing her arm.

"You are hurting me," she snapped, her gaze fixed on my hand.

"Sorry." I eased my grip. "I'm just surprised to see you here."

"The old woman is ill. I came to see if the doctors would give me some medicine." She held a small package in her other hand.

"They gave it to you?" The Army doctors weren't usually so generous unless they stood to gain something for their help. It put a chunk of lead in my belly to think what they might ask of a young girl like her.

She nodded. "My uncle. They gave it to him."

Surprised, I asked, "Your uncle—he's here?"

Another nod. "I must go."

"Of course. I will accompany you back to the camp."

With a giggle, she focused on me now, pointing. "Wearing that?"

I wore my uniform jacket with the sergeant's stripes.

"Better you not come now."

"I have questions for you."

"Come tonight—without the jacket." And she hurried off.

My spirits lifted. A stirring of hope. She seemed eager for my visit.

Aware of other eyes upon us, I turned and saw Tomas, standing with the soldiers down by the corral, watching us.

"This is the one you mentioned?" he asked, ambling up to where I stood.

"Yes."

"You're right. She is beautiful."

"Do you know her?"

He looked askance, an unreadable expression on his dark face. "You think I should know every Yavapai girl who catches your fancy?"

Chapter 8

Geronimo scowled, though he still motioned for me to take a seat next to him in front of his wickiup. Raising an eyebrow, he asked, "Has Turkey Gobbler told you to keep an eye on me?"

"No," I said, squatting beside him. "John Clum doesn't know I'm here."

Night had fallen by the time I made my way to the Chiricahua camp. The earlier sign of rain had filtered away, providing a warm and dry evening. The air was rich with the scent of cooking fires, sun-heated sand and unwashed bodies.

I saw no sign of Dee-zho-ne, but Geronimo and his family were having their dinner. Waving his women and children away, he'd beckoned for me to join him.

Gesturing with his chin in the direction of her wickiup, he said, "If I didn't know that one is the reason for you spending so much time in my camp lately I might not believe you."

He slapped me on the knee when I failed to reply. "A man should not be embarrassed to admit his interest in a young woman as fine as her," he said, following the comment with a guttural laugh. "Have you eaten, *Ne-chotay*?"

I told him I had.

"Some *tizwin*, then." He called for one of his women to bring it. I wasn't in the mood for drinking and it wasn't his company I sought. Still I couldn't refuse to drink with him.

After we'd toasted one another and quaffed the first bowl, I said, "Remember the rumors I mentioned the morning someone shot at you?"

A coyote yipped off in the hills and there came a rustling behind us in the hut where the women eavesdropped on our conversation while pretending to be busy with their chores.

"As I said then, there are always rumors. Many of our people would like to leave this place. There are always rumors of those planning it."

"This one appears to be true. Men intend on killing those who oppose running away as a means of convincing others to join them."

His dark eyes glowed in the light of the fire as he scanned me. "And you think I am behind this plot?"

"No. I think you are one of the targets."

Geronimo grunted. "No one has shot at me since that other morning."

"No. But someone has been directed to do so."

This resulted in a raised eyebrow and a peak of interest. "Oh? Do you know who this person might be?"

I nodded. "Me."

Geronimo burst out laughing, emitting a spray of beer from his mouth.

"It is a serious thing of which I speak."

"But, you?" he asked, when he'd quelled his amusement. "You are to kill me? Is that what brings you here this night?"

Inside the wickiup I heard the shocked murmuring of the women.

"Of course not," I told him. "I sought out these renegades to see what they plotted. They think I am one with them. That is why they gave me this assignment as a test of my sincerity."

"And what happens when you fail to kill me?"

"Then they will probably try to kill me."

"Hmph, you have been keeping bad company, my friend. What will you do?"

"I am trying to discover the identity of their leader. If I find him, I believe I can put a stop to their plans."

Geronimo paused for a sip of beer. "I hope you have allies to help you."

"I'm hoping *you* might be one."

"Me? Why should I help those who hold me prisoner?"

"Because you want to live—perhaps to run away yourself another day when it suits you."

Geronimo laughed. "You are a bold one, Ne-chotay. What makes you think I care what happens to you?"

"If you didn't, why would you have the girl warn me? I don't know why she would carry messages for you, but she told me the warning came from you. I think you might know more about this plot than you've admitted so far."

Geronimo's face took on a grim expression. He leaned forward and tapped me on the knee. "There are always plots, my friend," he said, "and there always *will* be until we are free of this place. You put yourself in danger for me the other morning and I have not forgotten you saved my skin another time.

For this, I am grateful. That is why I asked the girl to warn you. I know of this plot. I don't know who is behind it."

"But you seek to find out?"

"I do."

"Will you work with me?"

"No. When I learn his name I will deal with him."

****

I could have told him Chato was involved, but I didn't. It is never good to reveal all you know at one time.

I can't say I like Geronimo. But I do respect him. I was gratified he'd acknowledged my having saved his life. I wasn't sure how he'd felt about that first time until he brought it up.

It was last spring when he surrendered to Clum. Geronimo had agreed to a parley but told John flat out he wouldn't go to San Carlos. We outnumbered him and the small band of warriors, women and children he'd brought with him. Geronimo and his men had been relieved of their guns, though that didn't stop him from trading insults with Clum. The situation grew tense as time passed. Finally, Geronimo tired of John's insults. He rose and his hand went toward a knife in his belt. Without thinking of possible consequences, I stepped forward and took the knife from his hand.

I'm not sure which of us was more surprised when Geronimo allowed me to take his only weapon. Maybe he realized he had no choice. Maybe he was uncertain of his Power at that moment. Maybe he just didn't want to risk the lives of his helpless, unarmed little band of warriors. Whatever his reason, I knew I'd saved his life, and now, he'd acknowledged it.

****

Geronimo noticed before me that Dee-zho-ne had come out of the wickiup. "The pretty one waits for you," he told me. "Go to her. Her company will do your spirit much more good than that of this old man."

I didn't argue. I went to her. She greeted me in her soft voice and even offered me her hand so we could walk together into the shadows and away from the prying eyes of Geronimo and the elders with whom she lived. Her smile and the warmth of her little hand in mine sent a warmth of happiness coursing through my veins.

"Is the old one better?"

"She sleeps more calmly. The White Eye medicine is good."

"Your uncle must be a powerful man for the Army doctors to help him. They are not usually so generous with our people."

"My uncle is a respected man."

"Do I know him?"

Instead of answering, she tugged on my hand and drew me down an embankment where she reclined on a bed of fragrant reed grass. Below us the river, flanked by groves of willows and cottonwoods, gurgled over a bed of gravel. I lay down beside her.

"I do not wish to speak of my uncle tonight," she told me. "I think you like me. Would you not rather learn more about *me*?" Her cool fingers touched my cheek and my curiosity about her kinsman vanished.

"Should I believe you like me a little bit, too?"

In reply, she moved a little closer and our lips met.

What passed between us after that is not your business. Suffice it to say when I left her I was contemplating ponies, how many should be sufficient and to whom I should offer them—the old couple or the unknown uncle?

****

Immersed in these pleasant considerations, I was oblivious to others around me later as I headed back to my quarters until Cuchillo seized my sleeve.

"You were seen talking to Geronimo," he barked.

"Yes. Have you been spying on me?" I said it with a tone of amusement in my voice.

"It wasn't me. Others are watching you. This makes me look bad. It is because of me they've trusted you."

"How does it harm you if I talk to Geronimo?"

"You're supposed to *kill* him, not *talk* him to death."

I chuckled. "And I will. Have patience, my friend. Scarface didn't give me a time limit when he told me what I must do."

Cuchillo jabbed a finger at me. "You don't even have a gun with you."

"I might not use a gun. Don't you see—by talking to him I might win his confidence. Then, I can get close enough to use a knife or even strangle him. I don't think it matters how I do it. Just so I do it."

This seemed to pacify him. He scratched at his butt and nodded. "I suppose." He gave me a hard look. "Just don't let us down. That would not be good for either of us."

He stalked off into the darkness and left me alone again. I waited a moment longer, staring into the night, listening for unusual sounds. It might be dangerous for me to go back to the barracks if they were still watching me. I decided it might be better for me to seek out one of those abandoned wickiups and sleep there. I couldn't risk letting the renegades learn I was a scout.

****

I passed a long, uncomfortable night. The brush and bear grass covering of the hut had mildewed and its stench was enough to turn my stomach. The sleeping mat was no better, and I didn't even want to contemplate the vermin it probably sheltered. I had no blanket and I shivered in discomfort through the chilly night. Even had it proved more comfortable, I found it difficult to sleep, my thoughts drifting from the pleasant impression of my time with Dee-zho-ne to my fear of being discovered before I could bring the culprits to justice.

With the first light of dawn I awoke, stiff, cold and hungry.

Crawling outside, I greeted the new day, made certain no onlookers lurked about, then made my way back toward the scout barracks.

I'd only gone a short distance before being accosted by Rope and Dutchy. "You there," Rope growled, seiz-

ing me by one arm. "You're the one we've been looking
for. You're to come with us." Dutchy grabbed my other arm and they proceeded to drag me after them.
People stuck their heads out of wickiups to see what
was going on while others stood by, shaking their
heads sadly at how the scouts manhandled a poor
brave.

"Don't say a word," Rope whispered. "Al sent us to
find you. We were afraid the renegades might have
killed you and left you in a ditch." The grin he gave
me didn't make me feel any chippier.

****

"Rope got worried when you didn't come back last
night," Al said. "He wanted to go lookin' for you then.
I wouldn't let him, though I was just as worried about
you." He paused to wag a finger in my face. "You ever
do that again I'll personally kick your butt all the way
to Yuma and back. I don't know if you were shacked
up with some woman, carousin' with your renegade
buddies, or what. Next time you decide not to come
home when you're supposed to, send us a word to let
us know you haint been kilt."

I was grateful for their concern and embarrassed at
the same time. Much as I wanted to share the news
about my romantic successes, I decided now wasn't
the best time. Instead, I apologized for having worried
them and outlined my conversations with Geronimo
and Cuchillo.

"If I'd known a safe way to contact you I would
have. With Cuchillo and the others keeping an eye on
me I couldn't do anything to risk having them discov-

er I'm a scout."

"I warned you about diggin' such a deep hole," Al countered. He shook his head. "You keep playin' at this espionage game, I swear you're gonna either lose your scalp or your job as a scout."

I wasn't inclined to give up my investigation yet and I didn't believe Al had any intention of firing me. Not to brag, but a scout who can double as a translator speaking English, Spanish and the various Apache dialects has a premium. "I'm getting close, Al," I told him. "Don'tcha see? If I can find out who this Prophet fellow is we can stop the killings and corral these renegades. I can't give up now."

The bristles of his whiskers rasped as he rubbed a hand across his chin. "I suppose you're right. Just be careful. I don't want to lose my best scout and interpreter."

As I said, Sieber is like another father to me.

I gave him a grateful grin. "Mind if I get some shut-eye now? Didn't get much sleep last night."

Chapter 9

I had a good sleep—for as long as it lasted. It seemed I'd only drifted off to sleep when Rope shook me awake.

"Go away," I growled, plucking his hand from my sleeve. "I need my beauty rest."

"No denying that," he said, and chuckled. "But you haint gonna get it now. There's been another killing. Al sent me to wake you."

I sat up, rubbing my fists at sand-filled eyes. My mind lingered in dream-state, reluctant to abandon the fantasy I'd been enjoying of more cuddling with my love. It'd seemed so real I could almost swear I smelled her pleasant scent there in the room with us.

Rope tapped his foot impatiently, waiting for me to rouse myself. He grunted.

"I'm coming, I'm coming," I told him, throwing back the covers and planting my feet on the floor. "Where are my drawers?"

He handed me my trousers and went to stand by the door.

Drawing on my pants, I shoved my feet into my boots and reached for my shirt. "You said somebody got killed. Who?" I asked, as I buttoned my shirt.

"I don't have all the details. Apparently, Tomas

brought the news and Al says we're all to meet with Clum at his office."

"I guess we better get a move on, then," I said, ushering him out the door.

****

There wasn't room for all of us to fit in Clum's tiny office. He stood on the stoop as we arrived and the others—Al, Tomas, Dutchy, Crow, Alchesay and some others I knew less well—were in a semi-circle facing him. Rope and I joined them.

Clum wore a grave expression. "This is some nasty business," he began, seeing we were all assembled. "Tommy, why don't you come up here and tell them what you've told me?"

Tomas stepped up to stand beside Clum. He flexed his broad shoulders, then scanned his waiting audience. "You all know the old man called Piishii. It is him was murdered last night."

A murmur of shock passed through the group. Nighthawk was a respected leader of the Chokonen, Cochise's band of the Chiricahua. A famous warrior in his time, he had become a strong advocate for peace with the White Eyes in his later years.

"Who would harm this old man?" someone asked.

"I don't know who done it," Tomas said. "I was in the area when the tribal police found him this morning and they summoned me. Those police told me they'd heard the man being called the Prophet held a dance in the hills last night, but they couldn't find it. They believe Nighthawk went to talk against what the renegades are doing and they killed him."

"This time, they didn't just shoot the man," Clum said, disgust showing on his face. "The dirty bastards cut off the old man's head and stuck it up on a saguaro as warning to others." He pointed out at us. "We're workin' with the tribal police on this. Rightly so, the Choks want revenge. But I don't want their bloodlust spillin' over across the reservation.

"I want these scum caught. I want to find the perpetrators and hang every damned last one of them."

Most of us agreed that would be a fitting end for those who had harmed this beloved elder. We were as shocked as Clum anyone would have dared to do such a thing to Piishii. Even those who disagreed with his policies generally held him in favor as a man who wanted the best for the People.

After issuing a few more general orders, Clum dismissed the men except for Sieber, Tomas and me. He called us into his office for further discussion. I didn't know why Tomas and I had been singled out for this meeting, but figured it might have something to do with the shooting of the Pima. It did.

"I think I know now why Stockton was in cahoots with those Pima," Clum said once he'd seated himself at his desk. "But we're gonna stick with our story it was them killed him and not Tomas."

"What did you find out?" Al asked.

"Some of my informants down on that reservation claim those two *O'otham* scoundrels convinced Stockton they'd found gold on Apache land. Maybe they did, maybe they didn't. Maybe they just wanted to stir things up. Anyway, the plan was to kill Tomas and Mickey in hope of Apache retaliation. Stockton would then call in the Army and see that the Apache were moved off the land where they'd found the gold."

I scratched my head in confusion. "Didn't Stockton know—except for the renegades who ran down to Mexico—we're all on the Rez?"

"Except for the *Mansos*," Sieber said, referring to the "tame" Apache who lived near Tucson.

"Somebody said the gold is supposed to be on their land," Clum confirmed.

"Or maybe those sons-of-bitches just wanted to make trouble for our people," Tomas said.

****

Clum bade Al and me to wait while he sent Tomas off on another task.

"Al told me about your adventure last night," he said, returning to his desk. I expected to be dressed down as he didn't look happy about the news.

"Normally, I'd cuss you out," he continued. "But your association with these scoundrels might help us round them up—provided we can keep you alive long enough." He fiddled with a pen and tapped a finger on the desktop for a moment. "I guess the best thing would be for you to move into the camp while we pursue this. That way, they'll be less chance of you being recognized as a scout."

It seemed like a good idea.

"Geronimo and some of his cohorts know I'm a scout, but—" I began.

"Uh-uh," Al cut me off. "I haint gonna sanction you goin' over there where you'll be closer to your girlfriend. You might trust Geronimo. I don't. That's not the safest place for you to bed down."

"Well," I conceded, a little chagrined, "I guess it might be safer if I find a place to stay among the Chihennes. The Red Paint people seem to like me and my buddy Cuchillo trusts me."

Clum glanced at Al, seeking his opinion.

Al nodded. "That sounds like a better option."

****

Since they had "arrested" me this morning, it was decided Rope and Dutchy would escort me back to the Chihenne camp.

While gathering the small amount of gear to take with me—some clothes, my medicine bag and weapons—I filled Rope in on my adventure of the previous night with Dee-zho-ne.

My brother shook his head in dismay. "This woman is playing you for the fool you are," he said.

"What makes you say that?" I asked, scrunching up my forehead. I'd thought he'd be happy for me.

Rope sighed and shook his head again. "You still haven't even thought to ask her name and yet you're thinking about gathering ponies and seeking approval to marry her. And her *name* is the least of the things you don't know about her."

In the heat of the moment I'd again forgotten to ask for her name. "I'll find out her name and everything else I need to know soon enough."

"Maybe she'll stick a knife in your ribs before that."

"Why would she do that?"

Rope smacked a hand against his forehead. "Because you don't know a blazing thing about this girl.

Why is a Yavapai living with the Chiricahua instead of with her own people? Why is she carrying messages for Geronimo? And what about this mysterious uncle? You said she carried messages for him, too. He's supposed to be some big wheel over here, but you have no idea who he might be.

"I don't want to lose my brother because he's too stupid and blinded by love to ask questions he needs to ask."

His doubts made me angry, even though I knew deep down he was right. "I'll ask the questions when I'm ready. You don't know her. So don't go judging and worrying about something that's not your business."

****

Before we set off for the camp I told Rope to punch me.

"Why would I do that?"

"Because they're gonna expect me to have been roughed up since I was brung in for questioning."

Rope complied. I thought he hit me a little harder than necessary, but I guess he was still angry with me. Anyway, the bruise on my cheek and the split lip would help convince the renegades the interrogation had been legitimate.

The Chihenne averted their eyes as my guards escorted me into the camp. Rope gave me a shove that nearly knocked me off my feet and Dutchy aimed a kick that fortunately missed its target as they released me. "See if you can stay out of trouble," Rope growled. "If we bring you in again, things won't go so easy," Dutchy added with a backward glance as they stalked off.

They were well out of sight before Scarface and Cuchillo approached me.

"Dagut'ee," Scarface said. "You look like you had a rough night."

I fingered the scab on my lip and nodded.

"We saw them take you away," Cuchillo said. "What happened?"

I smirked at him. "What do you think? They took turns pounding on me, but I didn't tell them nothing."

"Why did they take you?"

I shrugged. "I guess they figured I'd been keeping bad company."

Scarface made a sound that might have been taken for a laugh. "But you kept your mouth shut about us?"

"Of course. Why would I tell those bastards anything?"

"Good man," Cuchillo said, slapping me on the shoulder.

I turned to him then. "Is there a place I can stay in your camp?"

Scarface scrutinized me closely. "Why here? Aren't you Bedonkohe? "

"I think some of my people have become suspicious of me. I think someone blabbed and that is why the scouts grabbed me last night. I need a place to hide out while I decide how to kill Geronimo."

"Hu! It is good," Cuchillo said. "I have a place for you. My wife's sister is a widow. She would be grateful for a good man to sleep with."

I raised a hand, horrified at the thought of him fixing me up with some fat squaw. "Thank you, my friend, but I already have a woman."

"A man can never have too many women."

"No, but this is one I hope to marry later, and I don't want to complicate things."

Now, it was Scarface who clapped me on the back with a laugh. "I think we can fix you up," he said. "There are plenty of empty wickiups in our camp. Come, we'll go look for one that doesn't have too many bugs. Then we'll have a drink to celebrate your release from those traitorous scouts."

Chapter 10

I took the first opportunity to sneak off and see my love. It wasn't easy. My new-found friends were anxious to spend every waking moment with me. I figured it wasn't a sign they actually liked me. It was more a case of them being suspicious of me or interested in how I planned on killing Geronimo.

As I stood before her wickiup, waiting for someone to acknowledge my presence, Geronimo came out of his. "She's not there," he said, coming over to me. "None of them are."

Stunned, as though struck by a blow, I gazed at him with a disappointed look. Had they run away?

"Don't look so glum," Geronimo said with what might have passed as a smile. "I expect they'll be back. Come on over and have a drink with me. I have some news that might interest you."

"Where did they go?" I asked as we settled ourselves on the ground and one of his women brought *tizwin* in response to his command.

Geronimo shrugged. "No idea. I saw her and the old ones leave this afternoon. They weren't carrying any belongings, so I guess they're coming back. They're not Bedonkohe. No reason to tell me their business."

I wanted to ask him why Yavapai were in his camp. Instead, I said, "The old woman has been sick. Maybe they took her to see the Army doctor."

"Could be," he said, pouring me a drink.

I accepted the drink, though I didn't want it. "You said you had news about that other thing."

He paused to take a drink before replying. "You want something to eat?"

"No. About the—"

"I'm hungry. Damn, I'm always hungry since we came to this place." He shouted for his woman again. I believe it was Chee-has-kish, the old one he'd married after his first wife was murdered by the Mexicans. She stuck her head out and asked what he wanted. I waited, impatiently, while she brought out several baskets containing strips of dried beef, roasted agave and nuts and berries.

He gestured at the food. "Help yourself."

Smelling the meat, a dog trotted over and began sniffing at the baskets. Geronimo clouted the dog on the muzzle with his hand. It yelped and backed off, but didn't leave, lying down just out of reach and whining in hope he'd relent and throw it some morsel. Even our dogs were thin and mangy from lack of adequate food on the reservation.

"You said you had news?" I ventured, as my stomach growled and I realized I hadn't eaten anything since noon. I took a strip of meat from the nearest basket.

"I've heard these renegades are a mixed group—not all from one band," he said.

That wasn't news to me. I chewed on the tough

morsel and took a piece of agave and a handful of berries.

"I've also been told this so-called Prophet is not a prisoner like my people."

I gazed at him, quizzically. "What do you mean?"

"I mean, he's one of you."

"A scout?"

"That's what I've been told."

"That's impossible."

"Why? The man seeks power. Are you scouts above such desires? You betray your own people to work for the White Eyes. Other than that, you're no different from other men in what you want. Why is it so difficult to believe one of you wouldn't want to be honored as a leader?"

He had a point. "Who is this man?"

"That, I do not know. He keeps his identify secret even from those who are closest to him."

Crawling on its belly, the dog sneaked close to the food again. Geronimo gave it another whack and the poor thing ran off, whimpering.

I munched the delicious fruit, assessing in my mind all the scouts I knew, and wondering which of them could be this mysterious Prophet. I couldn't think of anyone offhand. Most of us had been together for years. Many were related, or at least, belonged to the same clans. It was a puzzle.

****

I planted myself in front of her lodge and waited. And waited. My love and the old ones hadn't returned by midnight. Distraught, I trudged back to the Chihenne camp, intent on getting some much-needed sleep.

Along the way, I mulled another issue Geronimo and I had discussed. I'd finally come right out and asked him why a Yavapai family was quartered among the Chiricahua and, in particular, located right next to him as though deserving of his protection.

"No big secret," he explained. "Chali-pun asked me to take them in as a favor to him. The girl's father was one of those who died at the cave."

Chali-pun was one of the primary leaders of the clan. What Geronimo had referred to was the terrible incident in December 1872 when the Army trapped a large band of Yavapai in a cave in a canyon along the Salt. Unwilling to surrender, the people sang their death chant and charged into the waiting guns of the soldiers. Many of the women and children were killed by bullets ricocheting off the roof of the cave or by boulders the soldiers rolled off the cliffs. Seventy-six people died, and many suffered serious wounds. Chali-pun came in soon after that, because he didn't want to sacrifice more of his people.

Since her father had been among those massacred in this battle, she and her family should have been honored people. It puzzled me they had been sent to live among the Chiricahua and under Geronimo's protection. When I asked about it, Geronimo shrugged and said there were reasons. He refused to say more.

****

The bear grabbed my foot and tried to pull me out

of the wickiup. I kicked at him with my other foot and he seized me in a tighter grip, growled and tugged some more. A fog surrounded us and I couldn't see him clearly, but his rank odor told me he was a bear—and I was determined not to let him have me.

We Apache believe the bear to be one of our ancestors, which is why we don't eat his flesh. We honor him, but we also fear him. I struggled, hoping once he realized I'd never eat *him*, he'd lose his appetite for *me*. Sometimes outcasts and bad men take the shape of Bear, which is why we never speak his name if we can help it.

"Come on," a voice broke into my dream. "Get out here. We need to talk."

Rolling over and forcing open sleep-bleared eyes I saw Scarface hovering in the entrance, his ugly face scrunched up in anger. "You're a hard man to wake."

"You woke me from a sound sleep."

"I hope your dreams were good."

I didn't tell him what I'd mistaken him for in my dream. Coming up on my knees to face him, I asked, "What do you want?"

Scarface scuttled back so I could crawl out of the lodge. "You ate and drank with Geronimo last night like you were old friends," he said.

I blinked and threw up a hand before my eyes. The bright sun told me it was mid-morning. "I need some coffee. Where can we get some?"

"Never mind that," he said in his gravelly voice. "I didn't come to have breakfast with you. Answer the question. What were you doing last night?"

"Gaining his confidence."

"We don't want you to *gain his confidence*. We want you to kill the bastard."

"In due time."

He hissed and stood erect. "Your time is running out. If you don't soon do it, you'll find yourself a target."

"I need to talk to the Prophet." I knew I was pressing my luck, but what did I have to lose?

"About what? You don't *ask* to talk to him. If he wants to speak to you, he'll send for you. Just get the job done."

"When I'm ready." I turned my back on him and stalked off.

"Where are you going?" he called after me.

"I told you—I need coffee. Somebody in this camp must have some."

****

"You shouldn't make him angry," Cuchillo said, handing me a cup of the much-needed brew.

Squatting next to him, I blew on the coffee. It was still too hot to drank, but the heavenly scent proved enough to raise my spirits. "Why not? *He's* not the Prophet, is he?"

Cuchillo snickered. "Of course not. But he is hot-tempered, and if you push him too much he's gonna strike out at you like a wolf." He sipped at his own coffee. "Sorry I don't have any sugar."

I blew on the cup again and took a drink. "Ah, that's good. I'm just glad you had coffee. I don't know what I'd have done if I hadn't found any." After another sip, I continued. "I'm not afraid of Scarface. I just don't understand all the secrecy. If this Prophet wants us to follow him, why does he insist on having us get our orders from others? A good leader should face his men."

The Knife shrugged. "I don't know. It's just the way it has been since the beginning. He must have his reasons for keeping his identity secret. I've only seen him a time or two myself, and on those occasions, he wore a Ga'an mask. But I think you and me did see him without the mask one time."

"What? When was that?"

"That night we played the moccasin game. The big man who wore a hat and kept to the shadows. I never did see his face, but I recognized the voice. I'm sure it was him."

I remembered the voice had seemed familiar to me, too, though I still couldn't explain how. "Why would he mingle with us without the mask if he wants to keep his identity secret?"

He hunched his shoulders. "Who knows. Maybe he just wanted to spy on his followers. You want some more coffee?"

I handed him my mug. One cup was good. Two would be better. Who knew when I might get more? It wasn't like the Army would give it to us. The traders always had whiskey to sell. They didn't always have coffee. When they did, you had to have something to trade for it. And often, when you did get it, you discovered it was shavings of bark and not coffee beans.

When Cuchillo returned with the refill I decided to share with him one of the things Geronimo had told me. "Geronimo said he heard the Prophet might be a scout."

Cuchillo looked askance and shook his head. "That's ridiculous. Why would a scout want to encourage the people to run away?"

It was a good question.

****

Several times, later in the day, we heard gunfire in the distance.

Such sounds were always a worry to those who believed the bands had been brought to this place so they might later be slaughtered by the Army. Many people in our camp were nervous until word filtered down to us the soldiers had been called in to help the tribal police put down some Chokonen who had attacked a couple of Chiricahua who had wandered into their camp. It seemed the Choks wanted revenge for the murder of old Nighthawk and suspected the Chiricahua were behind it.

If the Prophet and his cohorts weren't put down soon, I feared we'd be in for even more trouble between the different bands.

Chapter 11

"I was afraid you weren't coming back."

She took my hand and placed it against her breasts. Through the thin fabric of the calico dress she wore I felt the warmth of her flesh and the beat of her heart, which seemed to quicken with my touch.

"Why would you think that?" she asked.

We'd come down to the river bank and sheltered under a willow. It was a pleasant evening. It seemed spring had finally arrived as was evidenced by the croaking of frogs along the river and the cooing of doves in the trees. There was a fresh scent to the water, the grass and the trees.

"I came last night and waited a long time, but you didn't come back."

"The medicine didn't seem to be helping the old woman. We decided to take her to see the doctor. He gave her a stronger medicine, which seemed to help."

"That's good."

"I'm here now."

"Which pleases me."

Dee-zho-ne rolled over and sought my lips. I had no desire to talk for long minutes as I tasted her sweetness. In such a situation, a man is easily led to forgo any curiosity about things not concerned with the immediate moment.

"I'm happy you missed me," she said, snuggling against me and breaking the silence.

"Are you?" I still could not believe one so beautiful found pleasure in my company.

"I coupled with you in my dreams last night."

I felt a stirring in response to her words and my fingers caressed her smooth thigh. "Dreams can be made real."

She smiled and drew my hand up to her cheek. "I think we should wait. My uncle would not want me to be that kind of woman."

The uncle. I'd almost forgotten about him. "Your uncle—I could talk to him. I don't have many ponies, but..."

A cloud passed over her face. "No. I don't think you should do that." She withdrew her hand and shifted away from me. "He is a stern man, and I haven't told him about us. Give me more time to prepare him."

"He is a man like any other. I'm sure if I talked to him—"

"No. Please." She sat up, turning her face away from me.

"What is it?" I sat up, throwing an arm around her shoulders. "Would he despise me because I'm a scout? Or, maybe he'd prefer a Yavapai man for you."

She wrested free from me, rose and ran off, leaving me confused.

I waited another moment or two, then followed. She had not gone back to camp. I found her seated on a stump a short distance away, crying and with her face buried in her hands.

"What's wrong?" I knelt beside her. "Have I done something to upset you?"

Her eyes glistened in the fading light as she stared up at me. There was a sadness I'd not seen before in her expression. "It's not you." She hissed a sibilant breath. "It's me. There are things you don't know about me. Maybe it would be better if you would forget me. I don't want you to get hurt."

"I would be more hurt if I couldn't see you and spend time with you."

Her fingers caressed my cheek. "I must go now. Maybe you should not come back here again." She ran off before I could reply, leaving me even more mystified about the ways of women.

****

I made my way to the Yavapai camp and sought out a man I knew. Charlie, as we knew him, had been a scout until he lost an arm in battle. His tribal name, *Inyaga Ahat*, meant something like Black Dog. Disabled, he'd been pensioned and had joined his people on the reservation. The man loved to eat and— I suppose out of boredom—gorged himself with food and became fatter every time I saw him.

Since coming to San Carlos, the Yavapai had dug irrigation ditches and become farmers, which meant they prospered and had more food than the other bands on the reservation. The Yavapai are strange people, not really Apache at all, closer related to the Mohave and Yuman peoples. Many have married into the Apache bands, though, and we can understand them, especially if they use the Tonto or *Nnee biyati* dialect.

Charlie, when I found him, was seated outside his wickiup—which his people called an *uwa*—feasting on a bowl of roasted rabbit, squash and beans. He looked up at my approach and grinned, showing small teeth worn down to nubs. "Welcome, my friend," he said in a high-pitched voice. "Have you eaten?"

"Yes. I'm fine." I took a seat next to him. "And it looks like you haven't given up the habit."

He laughed. "Eating? What better pleasure is there for an old man? My women no longer want me to bother them."

Aside from more weight and aging, he hadn't changed much from the last time I'd seen him. Unlike most of his people, Charlie was not tall and that may have made him seem fatter. He wore a kepi and a worn and faded Army tunic. Except for a breechclout, he was naked from the waist down. Creases in his dark skin bore traces of the paint these lizard people lather over themselves to protect against the sun and the odor wafting between us told me it'd been some time since he'd last bathed. "Will you drink?" he asked, licking thick lips to capture an escaped morsel of food.

"That, I will do."

Charlie shouted. A moment later, one of his women crawled out of the hut with a bottle of trader's whiskey. In accordance with their custom for married women, tattoo lines in blue ran from her lower lip down her chin. I tried to imagine my love with such disfigurement. I didn't like the image. When we marry

–I've convinced myself we will—I'll discourage her from doing it.

Charlie uncorked the bottle and handed it to me. I took a swig and handed it back.

"What brings you way over here?" he asked after a pause for a drink.

"I was hoping you might answer some questions for me."

His wide spread eyes were almost hidden under heavy lids. They peered at me now for what seemed a long time before he spoke. "What kind of questions? Do they have something to do with the rumors about leaders being killed?"

"Some do. I'll get to them eventually. First, I'd like to ask you about a Yavapai girl."

Charlie grinned. "You have feelings for one of our maidens?"

I nodded. "Yes. I believe I do."

"Hu! That is good. So, come on—tell me about her. What is her name?"

I bowed my head. "That is the problem. We have met and I think she likes me, too. I think I want to marry her. But I don't know her name."

"What? How can this be? How can you have feelings for a woman and not learn her name?"

"She is so beautiful. When we are together, I am so dazzled by her beauty I forget to ask her name."

"Hah! This is a real sickness you have my friend. How am I supposed to know her if you can't tell me her name?" He took back the bottle and quaffed a large drink. The liquid gurgled in his fat belly and he farted loudly.

"I'm hopeful when I tell you what I know you will recognize her. Her father was among those killed at the cave. Since coming to San Carlos, she has lived with the old parents of an uncle. In the Chiricahua camp."

He nodded now and there was a peculiar light in his eyes. "Under the protection of Goyathlay?"

"That is the one. You do know her."

"I know of her. I'm sorry, Mickey Free. I tell you, it is better you forget her."

"I can't forget her. I love her."

"No." He shook his head. "You must not pursue her. If you must marry, let me help you find another. We have many fine women here in our camp. I'm sure I can find a better one for you."

****

Trader whiskey is usually watered down. If it isn't, it may be adulterated with other substances you probably don't want to put in your mouth. Whatever tainted Charlie's whiskey, it had me bleary-eyed and stumbling as I made my way back to camp.

It's a fair distance to walk from the Yavapai to the Chihenne camp and, fortunately, the night had turned chill enough for these two things to have sobered me up a bit by the time I got there.

As I neared the first cluster of wickiups, the half-moon broke out from behind the clouds and threw a faint light over the path ahead. In the distance, I made out a figure seated on a boulder and smoking a pipe. Paying it no mind, I proceeded.

"Dagut'ee," I mumbled as I passed the smoker. He

grunted in response.

Darkness cloaked my surroundings again as the scudding clouds covered the moon. Behind me came the scuff of hurried footsteps. I started to turn and just then another figure stepped into my path. A skinny young man. He rushed at me, brandishing an ax. As he closed on me, I brought a knee up between his legs. With a groan, he sank back on his rump, both hands clasped over his hurt. Whirling, I smashed an elbow into the other man's face and heard the snap of breaking bone. But a burning sensation across one shoulder told me I hadn't escaped unscathed. Hands going to his injury, the second attacker dropped his knife. I saw a flash of anger on his face, then he turned and ran off into the shadows.

The other one was up and hobbling away, too. "Come back and I'll give you more of the same," I shouted after them.

Safe for the moment, I began to shake with an adrenaline rush. My shoulder stung, though a touch of my fingers assured me the knife slash wasn't deep.

****

I was doctoring the cut and grousing to myself about the big tear in one of my favorite shirts when Cuchillo poked his head into the wickiup. "Where've you been?" he asked. "I've been looking for you all night."

"Went to see a friend."

"Uh, thought you might have finally got around to killing Geronimo."

"No. Apparently somebody is tired of waiting for me

to do it, though."

He noticed the blood-stained cloth I wielded then.

"What happened?"

"Couple of braves attacked me." I chuckled. "I think I hurt them more than they did me."

Cuchillo shook his head. "I did warn you. The Prophet isn't patient."

"I'm beginning to see that." Tossing the cloth aside, I glanced at him. "Why were you looking for me? Going to warn me, were you?"

He scuttled closer, shaking his head. "No. I didn't know about the attack. I came to tell you something else. Remember how you said you'd like to see the Prophet for yourself?"

"Yes."

"Well—if you're still alive by then—you'll have a chance tomorrow night. He's called a gathering."

"Where?"

"He'll send instructions sometime tomorrow."

"And I'm invited?"

Cuchillo shrugged. "Scarface didn't say anything about anybody being excluded."

This news raised my spirits. Even if he wore his mask, there was a good chance I might learn his identity, and we'd be closer to shutting him down. I wondered how I might get a message to Al.

Chapter 12

Cuchillo and Scarface clung to me through the day. It didn't matter. Earlier, I'd entertained hope a scout would pass through the camp and I might have opportunity to get a message to Al through him. None came. And, even if one had, with my watchers I couldn't have chanced speaking to him.

After Cuchillo had left me last night, I'd discovered someone had been through my things. Nothing appeared to be missing and I assumed it must have been him, passing the time while he awaited my return. I didn't think the Knife was a man who would steal. Besides, I'd brought nothing with me worth stealing. In his boredom, he'd probably just satisfied his curiosity and affirmed his trust in me. Despite maintaining a friendly front, I knew Scarface and some of the others were less trusting.

I made no mention I'd noticed the disturbance of my belongings when the two of them returned in the morning. Cuchillo was his usual friendly self. Scarface was grumpy, and soon let me know the reason for his annoyance.

"Cuchillo shouldn't have told you about the gathering," he said.

"Why not? I'm one of you, am I not?"

"You haven't proven yourself yet. I don't know if the Prophet will want you there."

"We can ask him when we get there. Knife didn't say an invitation was required."

Scarface glanced at Cuchillo. "Sometimes this one talks too much."

"Look, what do I have to do to prove myself to you?"

His dark eyes bore into me. "Kill Geronimo," he said.

"Geronimo is a powerful man with lots of friends. I want to do what you ask, but I want to make sure I survive afterward. Can't you see—killing him isn't like killing some of those other old men no one cares about? I'll do it as soon as the right opportunity presents itself."

"It must be done soon. Some think you hesitate because you're not really sincere about doing the job."

"Is that why they tried to kill me last night?"

Scarface peered at me with a stern expression. "That was not sanctioned."

"What if they had succeeded?" Cuchillo said, coming to my defense. "We would have lost a good man because of their foolishness."

"A couple young men took it upon themselves without it being ordered," Scarface explained for my benefit. "They had volunteered earlier to kill Geronimo. They were angry you were given the assignment and their offer refused. You know how young men are—headstrong and impatient. They will be punished for their attack on you."

I grinned. "I dealt out a little punishment of my

own."

Cuchillo laughed. "I'll bet they were sorry they attacked you." He turned to Scarface. "Come on, don't be hard on our friend. What he says makes sense. Geronimo isn't just any person. This one will do it when conditions are right. I know him. He's a good man."

"I can be patient," Scarface muttered. "The Prophet might not be."

"Then let our friend talk to him tonight and explain his reason. His need for caution. He deserves to have that opportunity. What can it hurt to have him meet the Prophet and talk to him?"

Scarface relented. But I got the impression he still wasn't fully convinced.

****

After Scarface left, Cuchillo and I lounged around, drinking beer and waiting for time to pass. I was anxious about attending the gathering and getting a glimpse at the Prophet. Still I worried there had been no opportunity to inform Sieber. On the other hand, maybe it was for the best. If Al told Clum, the police or the Army might interfere, and we'd lose the chance to nab the Prophet.

"What are you thinking about?" Cuchillo asked. "You haven't said a word in the last half-hour."

I gave him a smile. "I've been thinking what a good friend I have in you. I'm grateful for the way you stood up for me, even though you knew Scarface might get angry over it."

"Ah," he said, waving a hand, "it was nothing. He

gets upset all the time. It's just the way he is. Don't pay attention to his moods."

"I mean it. I do appreciate you sticking up for me."

He was silent a moment longer, but I could tell by his expression he was pleased by my comments. He rolled over to face me then. "So, how're things going with that girl you want to marry?"

I sighed. "Not as good as I'd hoped. I just don't understand women. One moment she's acting like she loves me—then the next, it's like she doesn't want any more to do with me."

Cuchillo laughed. "Women are fickle. We only fool ourselves if we think we can ever understand them."

"I suppose you're right."

"I know I am. I've been married long enough to learn that lesson. Look, this sister of my wife is still available. She might not be as good-looking. But she can cook, she's still capable of giving a man sons and she's plump enough to give a man a good romp. Besides, in the dark, who cares what they look like?"

I shivered at the thought of what this woman might look like. "Thanks. I'll keep it in mind. I want to give the pretty one a little more time to decide how she feels about marrying me. Even if she finally agrees, I'll still need approval from that uncle of hers."

"You still haven't met him?"

"No. She keeps putting me off. Besides, I think he might be a scout."

Cuchillo sat up, gazing at me in shock. "That's not a good thing. What makes you think he's a scout?"

I told him about how her uncle had procured medicine and got the old woman in to see a doctor. "Not just any Indian can do that," I added.

"No. Still, it might not be as bad as you think. He could be a wrangler. You know the Army has hired some of our people to help care for the horses."

"Would a manure-shoveler have the respect to get pills from an Army doctor? I doubt it."

"Probably not." He pondered a moment, then added, "Maybe he's police. The Army might like one of them."

"You like the police?"

"No. Of course not. But they're not as bad as the scouts. I'd talk to a police before I'd talk to a scout."

I had a laugh inside, wondering how Cuchillo would react if he discovered I was a scout.

****

Dusk had fallen when Scarface returned and led us out through an area covered with cactus, mesquite and sage, and then several miles up a dry ravine surrounded by steep hills. We passed guards stationed at several points, though they didn't stop us or speak to us. I guess they must have known our guide.

Despite it being evening and cooler, I was sweating by the time we reached our destination—a narrow canyon hemmed in by steep, wooded hills. Several dozen people, both men and women, were already gathered, seated around small fires. There was a solemn air to this gathering, the parties mostly silent as though anticipating some miracle that would free them from whatever may have troubled them.

Scarface made his way into the midst of the crowd. Cuchillo and I hung back on the fringes. I preferred to stay in the shadows and my companion didn't seem any more anxious to make his presence known.

"Have you been to one of these before?" I asked.

"A few times."

"What happens?"

"Sometimes, the Prophet speaks. Sometimes, he doesn't even come, and other leaders bring his messages."

"But he's coming tonight?"

"That's what Scarface said."

A murmuring interrupted our conversation. A tall figure stepped into the circle of fires. He wore a black buckskin hood, which covered his face except for holes for the eyes and mouth. Like a traditional Mountain Spirit dancer, his naked upper body and arms were covered with sacred designs in white paint and he wore a buckskin skirt and tall moccasins. He raised his arms, invoking silence, though it already prevailed. Then, from a pouch at his side, he procured *hoddentin*, pollen from cattails, which he sprinkled over those nearest to him. Some of those blessed began laying gifts they'd brought with them at his feet.

A scrape of pebbles underfoot gave notice of more men coming up the trail below us. In the glow from the closest fire I saw one of them was Chato. Not wanting to be recognized by him, I moved farther back into the darkness. They passed without paying us notice.

"I tell you," the Prophet began in a sonorous voice, "I am he who has Ghost Power. The dead speak to me and they promise that if you follow me, good times will return to the people."

It was the usual mumbo-jumbo our people have heard many times in the past, yet in their desperation they continue to believe some shaman can magically make all their troubles disappear and bring back the good days from before the White Eyes appeared in our country.

The Prophet raised his hands to the sky and prayed for a long time. "Come, show yourselves to us," he called to the spirits. "White people are in the land that is ours. Tell us what we must do to rid ourselves of this curse. Give us strength to prevail against them."

Somehow, the voice I heard again seemed familiar, though I couldn't place it with a person.

After this long-winded prayer session, drums and flutes began playing and some of the people began a shuffling dance around the fires. Cuchillo, who appeared to be in a kind of trance, left me and joined in the dancing.

I moved around the edges, keeping to the shadows, but hoping for a closer look at the Prophet who was now surrounded by a number of men I suspected were the leaders of the renegades.

My attention fixed on them, I was startled when a hand seized my sleeve.

"What are you doing here?" a feminine voice said. "You must leave. If they find you here, they will kill you."

Dee-zho-ne gazed at me anxiously. "You can't be here," she said.

Chapter 13

"Come with me," I said, taking her hands.

She shook her head. "I cannot. But you must go. Go, now!" Still gripping her hands, I felt her quiver like an aspen leaf in a breeze. She scanned those around us. "Please. For my sake—go."

"Come with me," I repeated.

"I can't." Pulling free of my grasp, she backed away.

I hesitated. Was her nervous state simply fear I might be recognized? Or something more? "I'll only go if you leave with me."

Our voices had attracted the attention of some men. One of them walked over now. "Is this one bothering you?" he asked.

"No," she told him. "There is no problem."

He glared in my direction. He was a stern faced older man with hooded eyes and a broken nose. Scarface had told us weapons were forbidden at the gatherings and my guns and knife were in my wickiup. Yet, this man clutched a rifle in his hands.

"This is not your business," I told him.

We consider it bad manners to point at another person. We direct attention to another in a more subtle manner. This man did it by twitching his lips in

Dee-zho-ne's direction. "She is my responsibility. Who are you? I don't recognize you. I think you should leave."

"Please," she said, her eyes imploring me.

Puzzled, I told her I'd do as she asked. "But we must talk later."

She didn't reply. The man, who I now took to be her bodyguard, gestured with his rifle.

I turned to go and was confronted by another man. Chato.

He grinned, pointing a revolver at my belly. "Well done," he said to the other man. "You've captured a spy."

"Him? Who is he?"

"Mickey Free. A famous scout," Chato said. "The Prophet will be pleased we have caught him."

****

They led me back into the woods, Dee-zho-ne following meekly along behind us. I figured it would be only a matter of time until they killed me. Naturally, that wasn't something I wanted to contemplate but my chances for escape seemed bleak. I still didn't understand her role in all of this.

After we'd gone only a short distance, I saw the glow of a fire through the trees and heard the voices of men.

We came out in a clearing and found the Prophet, Scarface and several other men seated by the fire. The Prophet had removed his mask and I was surprised to recognize him.

"Tommy?"

His eyes flickered in the firelight as he gazed up at me. "Dagut'ee, Mickey. I've been expecting you. Come, sit by me."

Dee-zho-ne hung back, but I heard her crying.

Chato gave me a shove and I fell forward on my knees.

"Why are you doing this? You're one of us."

He barked a short laugh. "Only so long as it suits my purpose. We have been under the thumb of the White Eyes too long. It is time we show them we are not women. Did you tell Sieber about this gathering?"

"No. There wasn't an opportunity."

"We shouldn't believe him," Chato said. "He is a lying spy."

"No," Tomas said. "I believe he tells the truth about this. If he'd informed Sieber, the Army would be upon us."

Dee-zho-ne knelt beside me. "Please, Uncle," she said. "Don't hurt him. I will do whatever you ask. Let him go."

He wagged a finger at her. "Your foolishness brought on this problem. I will have to punish you, too. But first, I must deal with him. Now, sit over there and shut your mouth."

"She hasn't done anything. She never told me about you or anything else. None of this is her fault."

"I'll decide who's at fault. Scarface, bring the horses. And, Cuchillo."

Scarface nodded and rose, giving me a stern glance before heading off on his assignment.

"How long have you known I'd infiltrated your group?"

"For certain? Just tonight when Scarface pointed you out. I knew she was dallying with some man, but I didn't know who. I was suspicious when you told me about being attracted to a Yavapai woman. It shocked me when I realized you were talking about her."

"You didn't tell him?" I asked her.

"I couldn't tell him I'd fallen in love with a scout. He would have killed you."

"He still will," Chato said.

She reached out to touch her uncle on the shoulder. "Please, Uncle. I beg you—spare him."

Tomas backhanded her across the cheek, the force of the blow snapping her head around. "After all I've done for you. You dare to ask me such a favor? If you weren't my flesh and blood, I'd give you to my men for their pleasure. Now, get out of my sight before I beat you more."

Whimpering, she crawled away from us.

"That wasn't necessary," I growled. "She's done nothing to harm you."

Chato slammed the butt of his rifle against my head, and the world went dark.

****

I came to my senses, slung over the back of a mule, just as we drew up before an adobe shack. Chato dismounted from his horse, seized my belt and unceremoniously dumped me onto the ground.

I lay there a moment, breathing hard, as I sought to orient myself. My head pounded and my vision seemed out of focus. I couldn't be sure how long I'd been unconscious, or how far we'd traveled. My hands were tightly bound behind my back with raw-hide strips. I struggled to raise up on my knees and look around.

Slowly, my eyes returned to normal.

A pink glow in the sky to the east foretold the approach of dawn. Birds chittered in the brush. The shack must have been a long-abandoned miner's dwelling. The adobe was crumbling and one end of the brush and mud roof had collapsed. The gravel yard of the building stretched into a desert cloaked in mesquite, ocotillo, staghorn chollas, prickly pear and other cacti. To the rear of the building, rocky hills rose up to jagged red rock pinnacles.

Chato nudged me with a foot. "Get up."

"Where are we?"

"If I had my way, you'd be in hell with your White Eye friends. The Prophet says to keep you alive for the time being. Get up. Now!" He kicked me again, harder this time.

It took some effort, but I managed to gain my feet. A wave of vertigo took me and I staggered. A hand on my shoulder helped stabilize me.

We weren't alone. Cuchillo was the one who steadied me. Scarface stood behind him, a grin on his ugly face.

"Take him inside," Chato ordered.

Cuchillo guided me into the building. Rats scurried as we entered. The Knife seated me on a rickety chair. Scarface lit a lamp that sat on the table in the center of the room. As the light flared up I saw the small room was littered with rubble, the leavings of whoever had once occupied the structure along with debris from its decay. The room stank of dust, moldering trash and remnants of stale body odor. Plaster of the wall at the far end was stained yellow from water that had leaked in.

"This will be your home until we decide what to do with you," Scarface said. He struck me across the face with the flat of his hand. "I had a bad feeling about you from the start. I should have known you were a spy. You always asked too many questions."

"Maybe we're wrong," Cuchillo said in my defense. "I mean, the Prophet is a scout, too. Maybe Mickey—"

"*Don't you say anything,*" Scarface said, jabbing a finger at him. "This is as much your fault as anybody's. You were the one said we could trust this scum."

"Which proves you as worthless as him," Chato said, coming up behind Cuchillo and throwing an arm around his shoulders. He slid the blade of a knife across the startled Cuchillo's throat. Blood gushed in a spray that spattered both Scarface and me.

Chato released his victim. Cuchillo crumpled to the floor, kicked a second or two in a spasm as his blood spilled out on the dirty floor, then went still.

"Was that necessary?" Scarface asked.

Chato nodded. "No loose ends. The Prophet's orders."

"You might as well get it over with and kill me, too."

He kicked at me but missed. "You'll get yours soon enough. When I get the order, I'll take care of you. But it won't be as fast a death as his."

"What about her? What has Tomas done with his

niece?"

"That's not your concern, either. She'll get the punishment she deserves. Just you worry about your own hide."

"Geronimo will kill you when he finds out how you've betrayed him."

"That old drunk is going to die. Just like you. He no longer is worthy of my respect." Chato gestured to Scarface now. "I've got to get back. You stay here and keep an eye on him."

"How long am I supposed to stay here?"

"Until I return and say you can leave."

"What about him?" he asked, tilting a lip at Cuchillo's corpse.

"What about him? You don't want to keep company with his ghost, drag him outside in the bush. I got to go."

With a final glance at me, Chato strode out the door.

****

Scarface sat in a chair opposite me, sipping from a bottle of whiskey he'd brought in with him after disposing of Cuchillo's body. His drinking wasn't for pleasure. It made him drowsy, and every now and again his eyes would close and his head begin to nod. Then, he would shake himself and look about him warily. Scarface was afraid. I knew the source of that fear. To a degree, I shared it.

My only hope was to use this fear. Use it against him.

"He should have killed him outside," I said, breaking the silence between us.

"I moved the body as quickly as I could."

"That doesn't mean his spirit won't seek us. We are forced to remain here while Chato is gone. Chato doesn't care what happens to you anymore than he does me."

"Shut up. I don't want to hear your voice." The liquid in the bottle sloshed as he raised it to his lips again. Chato had left him a pistol. It lay on the table before him. An old revolver, rust along the barrel, one grip broken off. If I could get my hands on it...

"You know I speak the truth," I told him. "It will be dark soon. We should leave here. Maybe go up in the hills where the Chindi won't find us." As I spoke, I worked at the throngs binding my wrists. They were strong, but I hoped if I kept at them I'd find a weakness. As I moved my hands, a nail protruding from the rear of the seat pricked my finger. This could be useful. I rubbed the rawhide against the nail.

"A ghost can find you wherever you go."

"Maybe. Maybe not. If we hide and stay quiet..."

"Shut up! I don't want to hear anymore out of you."

He sat down the bottle and staggered to the door, looking out over the landscape.

"You know I'm right. We need to get out of here." I'd been rubbing the strips against the nail for what seemed a long time. Would it never break?

Scarface sneered at me. "I could leave you here for the ghost. I don't need to stay."

My heart skipped a beat. He could. His fear might persuade him to disobey Chato and leave me. I needed his horse. I wasn't sure how far from the reservation we'd come. My head still throbbed and I felt sick to my stomach. Maybe I was hurt more than I thought.

Scarface walked to the doorway again. "Did you hear that?"

"What?"

"I thought I heard an owl."

"I didn't hear anything." Our superstition tells us the call of an owl is death's messenger.

"I did. The ghost is coming for us."

"I hope he takes you before me."

Scarface rushed across the room, raised his foot and planted it in my chest. The chair tumbled over and I struck the floor with a thud. As I fell, there was a lessening of the tension of my wrists. The rawhide had finally snapped.

I rolled away from the broken chair, rubbing my wrists as I struggled to rise.

Scarface whirled toward the table, going for the gun. He pointed the muzzle in my direction and pulled the trigger as I clambered to my feet.

Chapter 14

The hammer clicked and I think we were equally startled as the gun failed to fire.

Not waiting for him to pull the trigger again, I plowed into Scarface, bowling him over. The pistol flew free of his grasp as we crashed into the table. The lamp and Scarface's bottle tumbled to the floor, both leaking liquid that ignited as the globe shattered.

The flames licked up the volatile liquid and sought other fuel as Scarface and I struggled within feet of it. Despite my injury, I had the immediate advantage of youth, his impairment from the alcohol and my own desperation. Sitting astride him, I pounded his face with my fists as the heat of the fire singed my backside. Thick smoke roiled around us, making it difficult to breathe.

I found his pistol, tucked it into my waistband and dragged Scarface out of the shack.

I should have left him to burn. As I sat coughing and spitting, trying to clear my lungs of the acrid smoke, he recovered and came at me again, drawing a knife I hadn't noticed from his boot. I raised the pistol and pulled the trigger.

This time, the gun fired.

The blast took him full in the chest and knocked him off his feet. A look of shock faded from his face as

I stood over him and he gasped a final breath.

The exertion of our fight and the effect of the acrid smoke I'd inhaled had weakened me. For a moment, I just wanted to sit there on the ground and recover my strength. Yet, I realized the longer I hesitated, the more difficult it would be to do what needed doing. Scarface's horse, tethered nearby, nickered in fear of the fire flaring up from the shack.

As I'd suspected, this was the only animal Chato had left behind. He'd taken Cuchillo's horse and the mule with him.

Calming Scarface's horse, I climbed aboard. I still felt the effect of that knock on the head and the exertion of my struggle with Scarface, but I knew I had to get going. I slapped the pony on the rump and we headed east, the probable direction of the reservation.

****

"I've got to make sure she's safe," I protested, struggling to rise against Al's restraining hand.

"Doc says you've got to rest," he countered. "That knock on the head scrambled your brains and all that physical activity afterward didn't do you no good. So, stop being pig-headed and listen to what's good for you for a change."

"But—"

"I'll check on her for you," Rope said.

His offer bought him a sour look from Sieber but, at least, he made no objection to my brother doing it.

"Geronimo has to be warned, too," I told them. "They're still planning to kill him. Since I didn't do it, I'm sure they have volunteers on standby. For all I know, it may be where Chato was headed. You've got to warn Geronimo. If they go through with it, the Army won't be able to stop the exodus."

Rope promised to handle both my requests and they left after I swore to follow the Army doctor's orders and stay put in my bed.

To tell the truth, despite my anxiety, I was relieved Rope agreed to follow up on my concerns and I could snuggle up under the blankets and relax. Reluctant as I might be to admit it, my ordeal—including the long ride back to camp—had taken the sap out of me.

Several times during the ride, I'd nearly succumbed to bouts of dizziness and weakness and almost fallen off the pony. Fortunately, that nag knew his way home and I stayed aboard by clinging to his mane for all I was worth. I maintained my grip and seat right up to the entrance to our compound where I apparently passed out and tumbled to the ground. Rope said Dutchy, who was on guard, found me and summoned help.

I owed him a beer, for certain.

Al and the others found it hard to believe Tomas was the Prophet and behind this whole crazy plot. When Sieber sent Dutchy to fetch him they discovered Tommy had fled. Somehow, he must have got wind of my return to camp and decided to make good his escape while he could.

I figured he'd be hiding out somewhere in the hills and not on the reservation. But, just in case, Al had our boys and the tribal police searching all the camps.

****

I felt much better by the time Rope returned, though his news didn't raise my spirits.

"She's gone," he told me.

"What do you mean *gone*?"

"Just what I said. Her and the old ones, gone. Geronimo said they must have sneaked off in the night. The wickiup is empty. Took all their belongings with them and went—God knows where. I asked around. Those who were willing to talk to me said they had no idea what had become of them."

I planted my feet on the floor and sat up. "Tommy must have sent for his parents after he left us up in the hills. I've got to find her, Rope."

"How? They could have taken off for Mexico for all you know. There's a lot of country where he could be hiding. We wouldn't know where to start looking for them. I understand you're worried about her. But she's his family. Surely, he's not going to harm her."

I glanced up at him. "I hope you're right. Tomas was pretty angry when he found out it was me she'd been seeing. He struck her and threatened her then. No telling what he might do if she defies him more."

Rope tapped me on the knee. "Don't worry. I'm sure she'll be all right."

I wanted to share his confidence, but I didn't. "What about Geronimo? Did you warn him?"

"Of course I did. I asked him and his family to come back here with me so's we could put them under guard. He refused."

"You told him about Chato?"

"Sure. Geronimo said to thank you for your concern. He said he already knew better than to trust Chato and has enough people around him he does trust. He said his power is stronger than that of this Prophet, and he isn't afraid."

"He has escaped a lot of bullets in his time. I hope he's right this time."

****

My worry about Beauty was consistent. Just because he was her uncle didn't mean he wouldn't hurt her. She remained vulnerable as long as she was with him. I had to find them.

I didn't believe Tommy had run off to Mexico. Fleeing might have helped him elude searchers. Still, I believed the man's desire for power probably outranked the need for safety. Having been a scout, he knew all our tricks and probably had plenty of allies willing to shelter him. No. I felt the man's vanity would keep him somewhere nearby so he'd be able to keep on with his plans.

The question was—when would he make his next move?

The move came sooner than expected, and from a different direction.

****

We were at breakfast the next morning when word came Geronimo was at the gate and wanted to see Sieber and me.

"What do you suppose he wants?' Clum asked.

"I reckon we'll have to go find out," Al said, flinging down his napkin.

"He didn't ask for John," I cautioned.

"Well, he's gonna get me anyway," Clum said, following us out of the mess hall.

There'd been gunshots during the night, but no reports of other killings, and it had been passed off as possibly somebody hunting. I had my doubts. Big game had grown increasingly scarce in the vicinity of the reservation, and hunting would have been more likely during the day. I suspected we'd soon know what really happened.

The three of us strode across the parade ground to the gate where Geronimo and several warriors waited astride their ponies.

"I bring you gift," Geronimo said, gesturing at a hooded and bound man slung over the back of one of the horses. Shifting his gaze to Clum, he added, "No talk to Turkey Gobbler."

"Too bad," Clum snarled. "'Cause I'm here, and I ain't leaving."

"Why don't you boys come on in," Al said, acting the hospitable host. "We'll find a place to sit and send for some coffee and biscuits and we'll have ourselves a nice gabfest."

The other warriors looked nervously to Geronimo for response. He glared a moment at Clum, then nodded and gigged his pony forward.

****

We took them into the now-empty mess hall and Al had the cook staff fetch a big pot of coffee, a plate of sourdough biscuits and a tub of grape jelly.

Geronimo dumped his prisoner on the floor next to the table. His escort immediately set to work slathering jelly on the biscuits and gobbling them up while the rest of us filled coffee cups and passed them along.

"Now, what's going on?" Clum demanded.

Geronimo glared at him, then fixed his attention on Al and me. "That one," he began, jabbing a thumb over his shoulder at the bound man behind him, "and another tried to kill me last night."

"Where's the other one?" Al asked.

"He wasn't as lucky as this one."

I reached over and pulled off the man's hood.

"You recognize him?"

It was the older of the two men who'd attacked me the night I visited the Yavapai camp. "I know him."

"Why have you brought him to us?" Clum asked.

"I brought him for Sieber to question," Geronimo told him. "We could have done it. I didn't think you'd like the Apache way."

Clum glowered back at him. "How do we know you're telling the truth? You could be behind this plot, implicating poor Tommy and others to conceal your own treachery. I don't know why you should expect us to trust you."

Geronimo grinned. Twisting his lip in my direction, he said, "He knows. I do not like this place. One day—when my people have enough guns, ponies and supplies—we will leave, too. But I will not kill innocent people to make others run away with me. Those who go with me will do so because they trust my power, and not because they fear my wrath."

Clum didn't have much to say after that.

Chapter 15

Our prisoner wasn't talking. It didn't surprise me. The poor man probably didn't know who to fear most—us, Geronimo or the Prophet.

"Maybe I should let you apply some of those Apache methods Geronimo was talkin' about," a frustrated Al said. He rolled down his sleeves and mopped his sweaty brow with a big kerchief he pulled from a rear pocket. Al had applied a bit of pugilistic encouragement with little to show for it aside from the bruises and split lip of his victim.

"He's not going to talk either way," I told him.

"I hoped I might convince him to tell us where Tommy is hiding," Al said, rubbing the knuckles of his big fist.

"He probably doesn't know. And, even if he does, he won't tell, no matter what you do to him." Apache are trained from boyhood to be stoic in the face of whatever trials life presents. We're expert at torture, but it offers our enemies little leverage in dealing with us.

Al conceded I was right and decided to turn the man over to the Army as Clum had directed.

I wanted to get out on the trail and search some possible hiding places. Clum frustrated that by restricting us to the compound while the Army scoured the hills. I had little faith in their ability to find an Apache who didn't want to be found.

****

Frustrated, I wandered down to the corral and frittered away some time helping the wranglers tend to the horses. It never failed to amaze me how currying and fussing with these animals could mellow a man's dismal thoughts and buoy the spirits.

Afterward, I wandered down to the gates of our compound and stared up at the conic hills covered with grass and shrublands, and the juniper and pinon woodlands beyond. We were days closer to spring as could be seen in the spots of green in the landscape, but a stiff breeze flung grit, demonstrating winter still wasn't ready to release its grip just yet.

I was still worried about Beauty, and eager to hunt down Tomas. I considered Rope's comment about not knowing where they might be. He was right. Still, I was confident I could find them.

It couldn't be done by standing here and gazing off into the distance, though.

I had to get out there.

****

"No," Al said. "You heard John's order. We're to leave the searchin' to the Army. If Tommy's out there, the Army will find him."

I grunted in frustration. "Those soldier boys couldn't find their boots in the morning if it weren't for the smelly socks stuck in them," I told him. "They've always depended on us to lead them where they need to go. Clum should know that. I don't object to the Army searching. But *we* should be guiding them."

"I'm sure John has his reasons for doing it this way. I don't want to hear no more arguing about it. Besides, you still got some healin' to do before you go galloping around in the hills."

"I'm fine, Al. I'm up to it. You gotta talk to John and convince him the Army needs our help."

Al grimaced and slapped a hand down on his desk. "*No, dammit!* How many times I got to say it before it penetrates that thick skull of yours? Now get out of my sight before I get really mad."

****

"He's right," Rope said.

I glanced at my brother in disbelief. I'd found and joined him out on the barracks porch after my conversation with Al. "You believe the Army can find him?"

"No. I agree about us sitting tight while the Army scours the hills. Clum's intent is to keep Tommy lyin' low and not launching any more attacks while he gathers intelligence on where the bastard might be hiding."

"*We're* his intelligence wing," I scoffed. "Who does he think is going to find the information if he doesn't send us out?"

Rope raised a hand. "Patience, brother. We'll be goin' out in good time. The fact that we're not out there right now is bound to make Tommy and his followers nervous. Hopefully, it'll make them careless. Or the lack of action on his part will convince some of those hotheads Tommy has lost his power. That might make one of them inform on him."

The gritty wind had abated and the temperature seemed more comfortable as a setting sun purpled the sky to the west.

"Clum tell you all this?"

"He did."

"So, he trusts you more than me?"

Rope shook his head. "He trusts you. Him and Al and me discussed this while you were still recuperating."

"How come Al didn't explain all this to me?"

Rope shrugged. "You know Al. He's a man of action, not words."

"So how long are they gonna make us wait before they send us out into the hills?"

Rope shrugged again. "I guess that's up to Clum."

"I've got to talk to him. I need to go back to the Yavapai camp."

"Why?"

"Charlie. I think he knows more than he let on when I talked to him before. I think he might have suspected Tommy was behind all this. He might be able to give us some idea where they're hiding."

"What makes you think he'll tell you anything?"

"Because he never liked Tommy."

****

As usual, I found Charlie nose deep in a bowl of food.

He was less enthused about seeing me and more

reluctant to talk this time. I didn't care. I'd come for answers, and wouldn't give up until I had them.

It surprised me to find John Clum more supportive of my intention than Al when I broached my plan to the two of them. Al, for reasons I suspected had to do with his fatherly affection for me and a desire to keep me out of harm's way, continued to be stubbornly negative about my leaving the compound.

"I think it's a good idea," John told him. "Charlie always liked Mickey. If he's gonna talk to anyone, it'd be him."

But, as I hovered over him now, Charlie refused to pay me any mind and concentrated his full attention on a venison stew thickened with ground acorn meal and a greasy cake made from the dried and ground seeds of the ironwood plant. Saliva ran down his chin and he wiped it away with the back of one hand before gobbling down another spoonful of the food. He wore the same Army tunic as before and seemed even fatter than the last time I'd seen him.

"I'm not going away, so you might as well talk to me," I told him.

Charlie raised his head and gave me a sullen glance. He wiped the hand across his mouth again and belched. "You want some? This stew is really tasty."

"I didn't come to eat. I came for some answers."

He gestured at the ground next to him. "Sit down and eat, my friend. That's safer than the questions you want to ask." He called for his wife and she came out of the *uwa* with another steaming bowl, which she handed to me. Sighing in frustration, I accepted the offering and took a seat.

I spooned up a bit of stew. He was right. It was savory.

Charlie's thick lips twisted in a smile. "You like my wife's stew?"

I nodded. "You know I'm still going to ask the questions, though."

Charlie sighed. "He's a bad man. I don't want to say something that'll bring harm to me and my family."

"He doesn't have to know where the information comes from."

"Hmph, he has spies everywhere." Charlie spooned up more stew, doing his best to evade my gaze.

"You lied to me before, Charlie. I don't like people lying to me."

His eyes raised a notch. "I didn't lie. I just didn't tell you everything I knew."

"That Tomas is the one they call the Prophet?"

He nodded.

"I need to find him, Charlie. Otherwise, none of us are going to be safe."

There was a long silence until he finished the last bit of his stew. Then he set the empty bowl on the grass beside him. He gazed at me, his dark eyes blinking like semaphore flags.

"You promise you won't tell who told you?"

****

Charlie belched again and lit a pipe before beginning the story he hadn't told me before. "Remember you asked why she wasn't honored as the daughter of one who was killed at the cave?"

I nodded, waving a hand to ward off the smoke from his foul-smelling pipe.

"It is because of him. He was one of the scouts who led the soldiers to the canyon where our people were hiding. He betrayed us to earn honor from them." Charlie spat on the ground.

"Surely you can't blame her for what her uncle did?"

"She was there. She saw what the soldiers did to her parents, her little brother, all the others. Why did she willingly go with him afterward? She should have despised him like we did."

"She would have been a child at the time. Maybe she had no choice. He is her relative. Who else did she have to protect her?" I hadn't been at that massacre, but I knew about it. Even some of the soldiers who participated were now ashamed of their actions.

The Yavapai had defied their attackers, showing their buttocks when ordered to surrender. Angered, the soldiers took their revenge by slaughtering men, women and even children who were trapped in the cave. They left the bodies of the dead for the coyotes and other varmints.

"She was old enough to know what he did," Charlie said, vehemently. "She could have stayed with us. We would have cared for her. Instead, she went with him."

"Why is she under the protection of Geronimo?"

Charlie tapped out the ash of his pipe and laid it aside. "That, you will have to ask him. I don't know."

"How long have you known Tomas was the Prophet?"

Charlie spat again. "He has always been a treacherous snake. I didn't know he was the Prophet until he came here sometime ago without his mask and began tempting our young men to join him. Some did, and others have indicated they will, because they see him gaining power."

Charlie hung his head. "I'm ashamed to say I've become a coward in my old age. When he first came, I told him to leave my people alone. He threatened to kill my family if I didn't keep his secret."

"It's natural for a man to want to protect his family," I consoled.

He shook his head. "I was afraid for myself. I should have told you before."

"Do you know where he might be hiding?"

Charlie lifted his head and grinned. "I have an idea."

Chapter 16

"Why is she under your protection?"

Geronimo stared at me without expression for so long I feared he might not answer. I'd stopped to see him before carrying the information I'd wrested from Charlie back to Al and John.

"You're sure he's the Prophet?" Geronimo asked instead of answering my question.

"I'm sure."

Geronimo wagged his head and scratched at his chin. "I'm not as smart as I used to be. I told you I'd learned he might be a scout. I never suspected it might be this one. I must be losing my power. I should have known it was him."

"My other question," I urged.

"You won't like my answer."

"Try me."

Geronimo pursed his lips and considered a moment. Then he said: "He offered her to me as a bride if I would protect his parents who weren't welcome in the Yavapai camp. I won't lie to you. She is so beautiful I was tempted.

"My women convinced me I already have enough wives. Still, I liked having her close by since she is so good to look at. I thought about marrying her to one of my sons. But then I thought it might not be a good idea to have a daughter-in-law so beautiful it would make me jealous of my own child.

"To tell the truth, it eased my mind when you came along and I saw you admired one another. I hoped you might remove this source of temptation—even though I admit I'd regret not being able to look at her when I get up in the morning."

His explanation made sense. I knew Geronimo to be a lusty man. Her beauty would have been a temptation too great for him to resist. Still, I was glad the temptation hadn't led him to marry her or give her to one of his sons.

"Wait," he said, seizing my arm as I prepared to leave. "Do you know where he's hiding?"

"I must go."

He scowled at me. "You do know. Tell me where he's hiding and I will bring you his head."

"I can't do that."

"He tried to kill me. You owe me the chance for vengeance."

I shook my head. "If you leave the reservation, the Army will punish you. Let us do our job."

"He murdered our people. Letting Clum hang him takes away our dignity. It is not right. If you know where he is, you must tell me."

I was tempted, but I resisted the urge. I had my own desire for revenge.

****

John Clum didn't like the idea, but Al agreed with me that ours should be a strictly scouts operation.

"It has to be this way, John," Al argued. "You know as well as me, the Army couldn't sneak up on a herd of buffalo let alone Indians led by a former scout. My boys know all the tricks and can get close to 'em before they even know we're there."

John only acceded when Al gave in and agreed he might ride with us.

Though he tried to hide it, we could tell Clum was excited about joining the mission. I think he'd got tired of the daily routine of pushing papers and arguing with Army officers and politicians and longed to get back in the saddle for some action. He traded his frock coat and tie for the outfit he'd worn when he brought Geronimo in without firing a shot—a fringed buckskin jacket, yellow gauntlets, and a turban-style fur cap.

I expected him to get arrogant and starting throwing around orders. But he didn't. I guess he didn't want to risk riling Al, and was just happy to be along for the adventure.

"Why do you think he picked this place to hide out?" he asked as we rode along.

"Charlie thinks he sees it as a sacred place where the ghosts give him power."

"Ghosts he helped create," Al said with a snort.

"Which should be a help to us," I explained. "Charlie believes camping out among all those ghosts will make his men nervous. They won't be as alert as they should be, and when we ride down on them they'll probably scatter like chickens before a diving hawk."

"I hope you're right," Al said. "These are desperate men. There's been enough killin'. I'd like to round 'em up rather than engage in another slaughter."

"If we put him down fast, I think there's a good chance of convincing the others to surrender. Tommy had a fair amount of people behind him before. His failure to kill Geronimo has weakened his power, and much of that support has drifted away."

"Charlie have any idea how many men went with him?" Al asked.

"Twenty to thirty fighting men at the most, Charlie estimated—a majority of them his own Yavapai people. Some boys and old men, and even the women might join in the fighting if they still back him and aren't too scared of the ghosts."

This meant we were pretty evenly matched in manpower, though I suspected we were definitely better armed. Our boys were all armed with trapdoor .45/70 Springfield rifles. Though single-shot, our weapons handled easily, shot well, and packed a punch. In addition to rifles, Al and Clum both carried Colt revolvers.

I doubted Tomas and his men had many firearms among them. Most would be armed with bows and arrows, knives and axes. An Apache can be deadly with a bow. I've known some to outshoot a man with a rifle. Still, the elements of surprise and superior weaponry were on our side.

Al snorted. "So we face the possibility of slaughterin' Yavapai at the cave again."

"Unless we can convince them to surrender," I told him.

****

Al halted our advance at a safe distance from the canyon along the Salt where we believed the renegades were hiding. The command set up camp and commenced to prepare a meal, which might be our last for a while, and a guard was placed around the horses. In the morning, our force would go on foot from that point. After we ate, Rope and I volunteered to go ahead and scout out the situation.

We'd chosen an arduous task. It was late-afternoon, the sun still blazing hot—and the terrain over which we were forced to crawl on hands and knees barren, broken with crevices, studded with cactus and jagged volcanic rock. Heat shimmered up from the sand and rock to scorch our hands and faces, so hot we felt it through our clothing.

We were forced to proceed slowly and keep a low profile because we knew Tomas would have sentinels on the watch. We'd had to leave our rifles behind, both because they'd be an impediment to our progress and also because the sun reflecting off metal might signal our approach. Rope and I both carried knives, and they would be our only defense if we were attacked.

For a long way, nothing stirred save for an occasional rabbit bolting before us or a lizard scuttling from our path. Once I came face to face with a Gila monster. Its beady eyes fixed on me for a long moment as its tongue flicked in and out, and I smelled its fetid breath as it debated whether I might be prey or foe. Its beaded hide rose and fell with its breathing, then it suddenly scuttled round and took shelter in a burrow under a cluster of rocks.

I crawled on.

****

The belief Apache won't fight at night is purely a myth. We are trained to fight at whatever time or circumstance is best for our survival.

Rope and I both knew if we were caught out in the open by Tommy's men we wouldn't live to tell about it. So, for the final hour of our approach, we were doubly cautious.

A sliver of moon had risen when we topped a mesa and came out in a small grassy glade overlooking the canyon. By the light of the moon and the glint of the stars overhead, we could make out the figure of a man seated on the edge of the precipice. This was the first sentinel we'd encountered and, fortunately, he had not detected us.

The guard seemed nervous, probably afraid the ghosts might come up from below and steal his soul. He paid more attention to what was happening in the canyon below than anything that might be creeping up behind him. This was to our advantage.

Rope, who was in the lead, crept up to the man, planted a hand over his mouth and sank his blade into the warrior's vitals. His victim made no sound and Rope rolled him over into the grass. I came up beside them and peered over the edge.

A number of women were bent over fires, preparing an evening meal for the warriors who lounged, smoking their pipes and conversing in front of hastily constructed *uwas* while children played around them. It was a peaceful looking scene, and it made my heart heavy to think of the destruction we would soon unleash upon them.

I gave a start as I saw Dee-zho-ne emerge from a hut and carry a flask across an open space and hand it to Tomas.

"She's with him," Rope whispered.

I didn't reply. My mind was fixed on how I might get her out of there before the attack. And I hadn't come up with the slightest idea of how I might accomplish it.

There wasn't a whole lot of time.

Even now, under cover of darkness, Al and the others would be walking their unshod horses up to join us. The plan was to attack just before dawn while the renegades still slept.

****

"Are you crazy?" Rope said when I broached my plan to him.

"I've got to get her out of there."

"And risk getting yourself killed—not to mention giving away our presence."

After the evening meal, Tomas had gathered his men around him and given them an encouraging talk. Then, confident there was no one around to hear or observe them, the people gathered around fires, passing time with a round of story-telling. A young man began tapping on a drum, and soon, some women formed a circle and started a social dance.

"Look, except for Tommy, most of them wouldn't recognize me even if they do see me. I can sneak into the camp, pass undetected amongst them till I find her. I'll bring her up here where she'll be safe when the shooting starts."

"You are an idiot, my brother. What happens if she don't wanna come? She's as likely to give you away as to come out of the camp with you."

"That's a risk I have to take."

Chapter 17

Ignoring Rope's whispered protest, I slipped down the cliff. Despite the risk, I was intent on rescuing her. Though I dislodged some pebbles in my descent and my breathing became as noisy as a steam engine with the exertion, I remained confident the Yavapai were too occupied with their singing and dancing to notice.

The dim moonlight helped conceal me, and I made sure to remain in the shadows cast by the hills around us once I reached bottom. I discovered my descent had brought me down near the mouth of the cave, a fact which kept most of the enemy at a safe distance.

A majority of the people seemed to have joined the dancers. A smaller group were gathered around an elderly man who entranced them with Coyote stories. Young and old, we Apache are fascinating by these tales of the Trickster who brought both darkness and light into our lives.

Catching my breath, I glanced around in search of Tomas and Beauty. Neither remained in the place where I'd last seen them. Tommy now sat across the canyon by a fire near the dancers with several henchmen who seemed entranced by whatever magic message he conveyed. My love was among those listening to the teller of tales.

She was not alone. She and an older woman—Tommy's mother, I assumed—sat side-by-side on a log, near enough to hear the stories but not in the group surrounding the speaker.

I needed to attract her attention and draw her away from the old woman who would be sure to betray me. Getting as close as I dared, I tossed a pebble. It fell short, the sound of its fall muted by the raised voice of the storyteller, the beat of the drums and the shuffling feet of the dancers across the way. A second toss. This time the pebble struck the sleeve of her dress. She brushed at it, apparently thinking it a noisome flying insect, and failed to turn her head.

With a sigh of exasperation, I stepped closer and threw another pebble, this one with more force than intended. It struck her on the shoulder and she whirled in my direction. Her face went white as she spotted me and she took a quick glance at her companion to see if she had noticed. Fortunately, the old woman remained focused on the Coyote story. I raised a finger to my lips and gestured for Dee-zho-ne to join me.

Gazing at the old woman, she shook her head.

I gesticulated again.

Her lips parted and a worried expression appeared on her face. She made a quick survey to determine her uncle's position, then whispered something to the old woman. The latter gave a nod of assent. My love rose and hurried in my direction.

Seizing my hand, she directed me farther back into

the shadows near the mouth of the cave. "What are you doing here?" she whispered, anxiously.

"I've come for you."

With a quick look back over her shoulder, she squeezed my hand. "If he finds you here he'll kill you."

"We've got to go."

"I was worried when they took you away before. He wouldn't tell me, but I thought they'd killed you then."

"His plan failed." I snapped a look at the old woman. "What did you tell her?"

"That I needed to make water."

"Good. We need to go. Now." I jerked my head in the direction of the cliff. "Up there. I've got to get you to safety. Men are coming. There's going to be trouble here soon."

Dee-zho-ne hesitated. Glancing back over her shoulder, she said, "I'm afraid there's already trouble."

Following her gaze, I saw the old woman had risen and peered back to where we stood in the shadows. Then she tapped a youngster on the shoulder, spoke to him and pointed across the way to where Tomas sat.

****

Seizing her hand, I hurried her back toward the cave. If there wasn't time to start up the cliff, I hoped we might conceal ourselves there.

There came a roar like a rush of wind behind us and I realized it must be response to Tommy's cry of outrage at finding me in his place of refuge. This was following by the pounding of many moccasined feet pursuing us.

We were nearly at the opening to the cave when my lover stumbled and fell to her knees. Her tight grip on my hand pulled me off balance, and only sheer luck prevented me from falling, also. "Leave me," she cried. "Save yourself."

This wasn't something I would do. Drawing her up, I attempted to move on. Again, it seemed luck and my having bent forward to help her rise spared me from harm as the blade of a tomahawk sliced through empty air where I'd been but a moment before.

The young warrior who'd reached us before his companions raised his ax for another strike. I'd drawn my knife and I plunged it into his belly now. He groaned and fell back as I withdrew my blade. Pushing her ahead of me, we resumed our run.

A rifle shot cracked above our heads. A warning shot, though the next might seek a target.

The moon had risen higher overhead, and by its light, I could make out the canyon wall. If we could scramble up and make it to some overhanging rocks just over the mouth of the cave we might enjoy some security. On that fatal day back in '72, some soldiers had fired from this position, taking a terrible toll of life on the trapped Yavapai. I hoped superstition would keep them from climbing up after us.

But my luck didn't hold.

Tomas and his followers formed a half circle, backing us against the wall of rock. Guns, bows, spears pointed menacingly in my direction.

Tomas, a stern look on his broad face, stepped out of the circle and came forward, moving as gracefully and confidently as a panther advancing on its prey. He carried a Springfield and, as he walked, I heard a click as he cocked the hammer.

"Kill me," I told him, "but let her go. You don't need her."

His broad mouth twisted in a half smile. "Who are you to speak of my needs? Maybe I'll kill her first and make you watch. In fact, that seems like an excellent idea. She has jeopardized my plans once too often. And you—you have been an impediment all along." He raised the rifle. "Drop that knife."

I obeyed. Against the odds I faced it offered little solace.

Tomas gestured for some of his men to come and take me while he held me at gunpoint.

They were interrupted by another unusual sound that caused us all to lift our eyes to the sky. It came like the sudden whoosh of a flight of birds through the sky, followed by shock on the part of the enemy as arrows thudded into the bodies of those around them.

The arrows were followed by the crackle of gunfire and more of Tommy's men fell mortally wounded. Those who survived, scattered.

Unabashed, Tomas raised his rifle, pointed it at me and pulled the trigger.

Chapter 18

"No!"

My anguished cry came simultaneously with his shot.

Just as Tomas fired, Dee-zho-ne threw herself in front of me.

My love crumpled and I fell to the ground with her in my arms. Men were slipping and sliding down the cliff behind me. Tomas cursed and moved closer. The breech of his rifle clicked open and he inserted another shell. I paid none of this any mind, my concern focused on her. She gazed up at me a moment. Her mouth worked, but emitted no sound. I felt her body quiver in my arms. Then, the light left her eyes.

For what seemed a long time—but was probably only a matter of seconds—I must have been oblivious to all around me. Gradually, I became aware once more of the gunshots, the shouts and screams of the dead and dying. What Tomas did during this period, I have no idea. Ample time elapsed for him to have reloaded and killed me, though he did not fire again. Perhaps he had been shocked by what he had done as much as me. He had threatened her life. Still, she was his flesh and blood and I didn't know if the threat was serious.

When I raised my eyes to look, he stood before me, holding his rifle at his side, a dazed expression on his face.

Another rifle roared, so close beside me I felt the heat of the shell as it passed by.

Tommy groaned and was flung backward as the bullet struck him.

****

Geronimo placed a hand on my shoulder. "Are you all right?"

Surprised, I gazed up at him. "Where did you come from?"

Geronimo grinned. "The people were trackers before the White Eyes created you scouts," he said.

"You followed us here?"

He nodded.

"Rope?"

Geronimo gestured around him. "Somewhere. He came down the cliff with us." Then, noticing the lifeless bundle still cradled in my arms, he asked, "The beautiful one..."

I shook my head.

"I'm sorry, my friend."

As the pall of smoke from the guns and campfires dissipated in the light of the rising sun we both noticed Tommy was not where he'd fallen. Geronimo thrust his rifle and cartridge box into my hands. "Revenge yourself. Find and kill the false prophet."

****

Reloading as I stalked across the canyon, skirting

the bodies of the dead and dying, I experienced a blood lust I hadn't known since the four raids of my warrior apprenticeship.

In times past, I may have considered capturing him and bringing him back for the Army to hang. Now, I wanted Tommy's blood.

Usen tells us to seek revenge against those who harm our loved ones, and we follow the path of Child of Waters who taught us how to deal with our enemies. My training as a youth prepared me for the task ahead. My legs, my mind, and my heart were strong. I would find and kill my enemy.

I have little memory of the next few minutes.

The stink of blood and excrement, the tang of cordite, these hung heavy in the air when I finally found Tomas huddled against a cliff wall. His face was drained of color and he seemed diminished from the confident warrior I'd known before. Yet, his eyes never flinched as he studied my approach.

His hair was matted, his forehead beaded with sweat, and his hands trembled as he raised his rifle to point in my direction. His checkered shirt was caked with dried blood, and as he moved, a fresh spill oozed from the wound in his side.

His rifle barrel wavered and I kicked it aside, placing the muzzle of my own weapon against his forehead.

"I want to know one thing before I kill you," I told him.

"And what is that?"

"Her name."

****

I can't say how long afterward Rope found me, again holding my love in my arms. Geronimo and his men had dispersed long before Al and Clum arrived. They'd left none of the Yavapai renegades alive, and their women and children had set up a terrible wailing as they mourned their loss.

With the rising of the sun, the air became tainted with the foul smell of spilled blood. Vultures wheeled across the sky overhead, and coyotes and other vermin skulked and snarled at one another on the periphery of the campsite. The canyon of the cave was once more a place of tragedy.

"What the hell happened here?" Clum asked as he and Al joined us.

"Geronimo," Rope told him. "He exacted his vengeance on the killers."

"He had no right. Where is he? He'll be called to task for this outrage."

"You sure about that, John?" Al put in. "He only done what we'd planned. Maybe he killed more of them than we would have. But it seems he did our work for us."

"He saved my brother's life, too," Rope said.

"Did he kill her?" Al asked, nodding at Dee-zho-ne.

"No," I told him. "She took a bullet Tomas meant for me. Geronimo got him right after that." Let them think Geronimo had killed Tommy. I wasn't ready to admit my bloodlust had rivaled my sense of duty.

****

I was oblivious to much of what happened afterward. The bodies of the fallen were buried and the surviving women and children were rounded up and escorted back to the reservation. Once back in our quarters, Al and the others left me to my own mourning. Life had lost its attraction, and I drifted through the next few days in a fog of depression and dissolution. I sought solace in drink and found none. Time passed and I took no notice of it, sitting for long hours staring into space, or wandering in the surrounding desert, seeking no company and declining to listen to any words of comfort.

One morning as I passed Al's office, a familiar figure came out of the building and stood watching my approach.

Chato.

"What are you doing here?" I demanded.

"I've joined the scouts," he said, giving me a broad grin.

"What? Sieber approved this?"

Chato leaned on the porch railing and peered at me with an insolent sneer. "I think he is glad to have me. He knows I am a warrior with great power."

I could not believe Al had accepted this viper into our nest. Had he forgotten Chato had conspired with Tomas and his crew, and probably had been responsible for some of the murders that had taken place?

I skirted around him, intent on giving Al a piece of my mind.

Chato stopped me with a hand on my shoulder. "You and I could be great friends," he said. "I have much power. I could be a better friend to you than Geronimo has been."

I shook off his grip. "You will never be the man Geronimo is."

Al looked up as I entered, slamming the door behind me. He sat with his feet propped up on the desk and his nose buried in a newspaper. I saw by the date it was an old issue though the age of these sheets didn't seem to matter to Al and Clum who passed them back and forth until the papers were in tatters and they'd absorbed every item of interest.

"Well, you don't look any happier than when you left," he said, turning a page.

"You accepted Chato as a scout."

He ignored me for a moment while he finished reading a column. Then, replied with a laconic, "Yep."

"Why in hell would you do that?"

Al lifted his gaze to me, tugged on his mustache and grinned. "You think of a better way to keep an eye on him?"

Chapter 19

We do not speak the names of the dead. Yet, it was in death that I finally had her name. Though I will not speak it, I cherish it. She is in the Happy Place and I am left with only her name, memory, and imagining of what we might have had together.

I know Rope and Al worried about me and did their best to keep an eye on me, though I shook off even their companionship.

Nothing got through to me until the morning Geronimo came and talked sense to me.

As on previous days, I'd sought solitude, shuffling out past the gates to find a seat on a sun-warmed boulder, staring into the slow moving waters of the Gila. I'd carried a bottle with me, but it sat uncorked, on my lap, as my mind wandered with the sound of the stream and the birds flittering and chattering in the cottonwoods around me.

Geronimo came silently and seated himself beside me on the rock. For a time, he said nothing and I paid him no heed, hoping he would take the hint I sought no company.

"You will not find her here," he said, finally.

I peered at him, but made no reply.

He sat as though carved of stone, a sturdy man

clad in a faded muslin shirt, breechclout and boot-moccasins, those obsidian eyes staring back at me, unflinching, no expression lighting his stern face.

"Once, like you, I lost a woman who warmed and lighted my soul like sunlight," he said.

I knew he spoke of Alope, his first wife, who had been murdered down in Mexico.

"When I lost her, I thought I could no longer live. Like you, I sat for days, staring into the dark waters of a river, unable to find myself."

The story was familiar to me. Geronimo, then known as Goyathlay, had gone with others to trade with friendly Mexicans in the town of Janos. While they were gone, another band of Mexicans attacked the camp, killing many, including his mother, wife and children, and carrying others off as slaves.

"Her father didn't like me and demanded more po-nies than he thought I could gather," Geronimo said, reflecting on a memory he seldom shared with others. "I would have gladly given more—because she had taken my heart and I needed her by my side," he told me now. "We were happy for a short time, and she gave me three children. Life was perfect, and I thought nothing could ever change it.

"When those Mexicans took my family from me, it was as though they had killed me, too. Everything that had meaning for me had gone. I had no desire to eat, to drink, or even to fight. I was dead. Nothing mattered to me."

I knew exactly what he meant. I felt the same way, though she and I had been robbed of the chance to even marry. He'd primed my interest. Curious, I asked how he'd finally coped. "What did you do? I can't think of anything that will carry away the pain."

"I felt the same. Like you, I mourned. Then, against the advice of others, I went back to our camp. I was told the Mexicans might be waiting there to trap more of us. And, even if they weren't, the Chindi, the ghosts, would be at that place.

"I didn't fear the ghost sickness. How could it be any worse than what I already felt? I went and I found the bodies of my mother, my children and my love. The Mexicans had defiled them, cutting off their hair—even that of the children—and the ground was stained black with their blood.

"I sat with their bodies, my face in my hands as I wept, feeling even more alone as I waited for the ghosts to take me. I didn't care what happened to me."

Geronimo ceased speaking. He peered at me, tears in his dark eyes.

The old stories came back to me. "That's when you got your power, isn't it?"

He nodded. "A voice called my name. At first, I thought I'd gone mad with grief. I ignored it. It called again, and again. Only when it called for the fourth time—the sacred number—did I realize I must answer."

"It might have been a Chindi, trying to fool you."

"But it wasn't. It may have been a Ga'an or even come from Usen. The source didn't matter. The voice gave me the Power. It told me the enemies' bullets could not harm me, and they could not stand against my arrows. I knew I was destined to use this Power to revenge myself on those who'd taken away my happiness."

This was when Goyathlay became Geronimo—an avenger many would follow wherever he might lead.

He reached out, now, and laid a hand on my knee. "I'm sorry for your loss."

I nodded.

"One more thing you must hear, Ne-chotay. Your life has not ended. She would not want that for you. The beautiful one would want you to go forth and find a new happiness."

"Not easy to do," I muttered, glumly.

"True. Yet it is what you *must* do."

****

A month passed and hardly a day went by that I didn't miss her and mourn for what we might have had. Rope and Al continued to worry about me, and I appreciated their concern. I tried to put on a good front when they were around, though I wasn't fooling them.

At Al's insistence, Rope took me off the reservation for a hunting trip. It was intended to take my mind off my loss. It didn't but, again, I appreciated the gesture. I did enjoy Rope's company. It was good to be in the hills with no duty but to stalk the game we sought, take pleasure in the beauty of what Usen had provided for us, and express gratitude for the joy of life.

We returned, tired, dirty and with a good supply of smoked meat—deer, elk and javelina. We'd eaten good on the trip, and couldn't stand to see the faces of the hungry old ones and children. It made our hearts feel good to distribute all that meat to people in the camps.

Life was not the same. Nothing will ever be the same. But, as Geronimo had assured me, time spreads out before me. She would want me to enjoy it. I will try—for her sake, as much as my own.

Author's Note:

This is a true story—except for the parts that are fiction.

Mickey Free, Geronimo, Sieber, Rope, Clum and some others did exist. The Prophet, Beauty and others are products of my imagination. The events depicted—save for the original massacre at the cave and the murder of Geronimo's first wife—are also products of my imagination...though I've tried to be true to the possibility.

Some years after the time of my story, Noch-ay-del-klinne, a Prophet who had been a scout, did stir up the People and may have influenced Geronimo's decision to leave San Carlos in 1878. Disgusted with treatment of the People, Clum had gone on to other pursuits a year earlier, leaving a much weaker agent in charge of the reservation.

Geronimo would break out and return several more times before his final surrender in 1886.

Though never really friends, some sources indicate Geronimo believed Mickey Free and Chato told lies that influenced Army behavior toward him. Ironically, Chato became a scout and General George Crook credited him with an influential role in Geronimo's final surrender. Despite his service to the Army, Chato was arrested and deported to Florida along with Geronimo and other Apache in 1886.

About the Author

A retired newspaper editor, J. R. Lindermuth is the author of 15 novels and a non-fiction regional history. Since retiring, he has served as librarian of his county historical society where he assists patrons with genealogy and research. He lives and writes in a house built by a man who rode with Buffalo Bill Cody. His short stories have appeared in a variety of magazines. He is a member of International Thriller Writers and the Short Mystery Fiction Society, where he served a term as vice president. You are invited to visit his website at: http://www.jrlindermuth.net.

ONE-EYED COWBOY WILD—John Nesbitt
TWIN RIVERS—John Nesbitt
WILD ROSE OF RUBY CANYON— John Nesbitt
SILENCE RIDES ALONE— Charles Millsted
TRIPLE SHOT WESTERNS—John Nesbitt, Kevin
Crisp, and Les Williams
HALFBREED LAW—Chuck Tyrell
ONCE A DROVER—Jerry Guin
THE PEACEMAKER—Andrew McBride
THE HALF-BREED GUNSLINGER—Bret Lee Hart
SOUTH OF RISING SUN—John McCall
TROUBLE AT TIMBER RIDGE—Kevin Crisp
SUNDOWN WESTERN TALES—Max Brand, Charlie
Steel, Zane Grey, Gordon L. Rottman, Richard Pro-
sch, Kyle Rudek, W.M. Shockley, Robert Steele, Big
Jim Williams, and Lane Pierce
THE DUNDEE SAGA, BOOK 1: TUCSON—Kit Prate
THE DUNDEE SAGA, BOOK 2: CASA GRANDE—
Kit Prate
THE OUTLAW, BILLY STARBUCK—Kit Prate
THE DOCTOR'S BAG: MEDICINE AND SURGERY
OF YESTERYEAR—Dr. Keith Souter
www.sundownpress.com